'It's lovely and cool. Why don't you come in?'

Emma looked at him as though he were mad.

'Come in?' she asked. 'With you?'

He nodded. He was already regretting the invitation. It had just slipped out—a manifestation of his subconscious and the part of him that wanted her naked in the water with him.

'That would be scandalous.'

Seb shrugged. 'There's no one here to tell.'

Emma looked around her, just to confirm they were alone.

'I won't look as you get in,' Seb said. 'On my honour.'

Emma slipped off her heavy boots and cautiously dipped a toe into the water. Seb could tell it must feel heavenly against her skin as she sighed and closed her eyes.

'I suppose if you s   half   '

Seb grinned. She   e should be a gent   t, then turn his bac   e wasn't that strong   e nothing more than the cool water between their bodies.

'Turn   ing.'

NEWHAM LIBRARIES

90800100241596

AUTHOR NOTE

Egypt has always seemed one of the most romantic of countries to me. Steeped in history, it is a country of extremes, with the lush lands surrounding the Nile contrasting starkly with the barren desert. Ever since visiting Egypt I've wanted to return. I want to gaze again on the magnificent temples, the hidden tombs, and soak up the culture and atmosphere of such an inspiring country. In writing *Under a Desert Moon* I got my opportunity to return at least in mind—if not in body.

I decided to set *Under a Desert Moon* in the late Regency period because, to me, this was an exciting time for Egyptian archaeology. Tutankhamun's tomb was still over half a century away from being discovered, but the wider world was just beginning to become interested in the secrets Egypt's past had to offer. European academics and archaeologists had just started to arrive in Egypt and bring with them the curiosity of their countrymen back home. It was a time when anything could happen; tombs and temples that no one had set foot in for thousands of years were being unearthed.

I couldn't think of a more perfect setting for Seb and Emma's blossoming romance.

UNDER A
DESERT MOON

Laura Martin

All rights reserved including the right of reproduction in whole
or in part in any form. This edition is published by arrangement with
Harlequin Books S.A.

This is a work of fiction. Names, characters, places, locations and
incidents are purely fictional and bear no relationship to any real
life individuals, living or dead, or to any actual places, business
establishments, locations, events or incidents. Any resemblance is
entirely coincidental.

This book is sold subject to the condition that it shall not, by way of
trade or otherwise, be lent, resold, hired out or otherwise circulated
without the prior consent of the publisher in any form of binding or
cover other than that in which it is published and without a similar
condition including this condition being imposed on the subsequent
purchaser.

® and TM are trademarks owned and used by the trademark owner
and/or its licensee. Trademarks marked with ® are registered with the
United Kingdom Patent Office and/or the Office for Harmonisation in
the Internal Market and in other countries.

Published in Great Britain 2015
by Mills & Boon, an imprint of Harlequin (UK) Limited,
Eton House, 18-24 Paradise Road, Richmond, Surrey, TW9 1SR

© 2015 Laura Martin

ISBN: 978-0-263-24797-8

Harlequin (UK) Limited's policy is to use papers that are natural,
renewable and recyclable products and made from wood grown in
sustainable forests. The logging and manufacturing processes conform
to the legal environmental regulations of the country of origin.

Printed and bound in Spain
by CPI, Barcelona

Laura Martin writes historical romances with an adventurous undercurrent. When not writing she spends her time working as a doctor in Cambridgeshire, where she lives with her husband. In her spare moments Laura loves to lose herself in a book, and has been known to read cover to cover in a single day when the story is particularly gripping. She also loves to travel, especially visiting historical sites and far-flung shores.

**Visit the author profile page
at millsandboon.co.uk**

For Mum, for all those holidays and trips
to see piles of old rocks.
And for Luke. You make me love you more
every single day.

Chapter One

Emma leaned over the side of the boat and allowed her fingers to trail across the surface of the water. It was cool against her skin, a refreshing sensation in the heat of the afternoon sun.

'Careful,' Ahmed said gently. 'You wouldn't want the crocodiles to bite those fingers off.'

Emma withdrew her fingers from the water immediately and peered suspiciously into the murky depths. She glanced at Ahmed and wondered if the older man was teasing her. She knew the Nile was overrun with the vicious reptiles, but surely one wouldn't be bold enough to approach their little group of feluccas.

'Crocodiles are fearless creatures,' Ahmed said, as if reading her mind. 'They've been known to attack flotillas if the temptation is right.'

Emma shifted away from the side of the felucca and forced her gaze up from the water.

'Only a few more minutes,' Ahmed said, settling back in the shade and closing his eyes. 'Keep watching the left bank.'

She scanned the sloping bank for any sign of civilisation. They were only an hour away from Cairo, their final destination, but for now Emma was much more interested in what lay around the next bend in the river.

'The Temple of Horus,' she whispered, as they rounded the natural curve and the rolling landscape gave way to the sharp lines of a man-made structure. It was magnificent. The sand-coloured columns rose skywards and as they drew closer she could even see statues of the hawk-headed god Horus flanking the entrance to the temple.

'Have we not got time to stop?' Emma asked wistfully, already knowing the answer to her question.

They had been sailing down the Nile for ten days, a trip that was only meant to take eight. The owner of this little group of feluccas had been patient at first, indulging her requests that they stop at each ruined monument that sat near the river, but she knew he would not tolerate any further delay.

Ahmed spoke to the owner in rapid Arabic whilst Emma tried to plaster her most gracious smile on her face.

She followed the heated exchange and only let out the breath she had been holding when Ahmed returned, shaking his head.

'He says no. Regretfully they cannot make any more stops.'

Emma doubted he had been that polite.

'But it's the Temple of Horus,' she argued.

'You will have plenty of time to visit temples and tombs, *sitt*,' Ahmed said, using the Arabic title of respect to address her. 'This is just the beginning.'

Emma knew he was right, but still she couldn't tear her eyes away from the majestic temple. This was her dream, her fantasy. Whilst other girls had dreamed of rich husbands and fancy titles, Emma had longed for the exotic. Her father was a celebrated Egyptologist and for many years he'd lived in Cairo Throughout Emma's childhood he'd regaled her with tales of the pharaohs, myths about the Egyptian gods and descriptions of the modern-day Egypt. For all her life Emma had wanted to see it all for herself, and now she was here.

Instinctively Emma's fingers closed around the delicate scroll that was hidden in the folds of her skirt. She would have her adventure soon enough, and the Temple of Horus would pale in comparison to the delights she would discover when she followed the map on the scroll.

A movement in the distance caught her eye and Emma squinted into the late afternoon sun. Something was moving at great speed through the temple. She sat a little straighter and strained her eyes, trying to work out exactly what it was.

A man. She was sure of it. There was a man running through the temple at such a speed it was as though his life depended on it. She looked around to see if anyone else had noticed. Ahmed was doing his best impression of a man asleep and the owner of the felucca was looking ahead, ignoring the spectacular temple to his left.

Emma watched as the figure sprinted out between two statues of Horus and started to slide down the bank towards the river. A second later it became apparent why he was running so fast. Six men, dressed in the traditional long white robes of the Egyptians, exploded out of the temple's entrance, shouting in Arabic and gesturing angrily. Emma was surprised to see they all had long, curved swords, which they were brandishing in the air in a rather alarming manner.

The first man had reached the bottom of the slope and took a second to glance over his shoulder. His pursuers were just starting the descent. In a matter of seconds they would be upon him. He looked from left to right, seeming to realise he was running out of options. Suddenly he looked up slightly and his eyes met Emma's over the shimmering surface of the Nile. He paused, grinned and winked at her.

Emma's eyes widened. She didn't think she'd ever been winked at before. She knew she should be affronted but she couldn't tear her gaze away from the man. She watched as he tucked whatever he was carrying into his satchel and dived into the fast-flowing waters of the Nile.

Emma held her breath. It seemed as if he was under the water for ages and she scanned the surface for any sign of life. Panic gripped her as she wondered if he'd been swept away by the current, or, worse, eaten by a crocodile. She redoubled her efforts in looking, dreading the thought that she might see a crimson slash of blood stain the blue waters of the Nile.

'Permission to come aboard?' a low voice asked close to her ear.

Emma jumped so much she nearly fell overboard.

She looked down, surprised to see the man she had been watching for had surfaced so close to the boat. He must have swum the entire way under the water.

He grinned at her and she found herself smiling back.

With strong arms he hauled himself up over the side of the felucca and collapsed onto the deck.

Mohammed, the owner of the felucca, was by his side in a second and Emma let out a little gasp of surprise as he drew his sword and held it to the man's throat.

'Filthy English grave robber,' he said in heavily accented English. 'I should throw you back overboard and let the crocodiles have you.'

'You will not,' Emma said, surprising herself with the force of her voice.

Mohammed, Ahmed and the Englishman turned to her in surprise.

'You heard the lady,' the Englishman said. 'I have a protector.'

Emma's eyes narrowed. She thought she'd detected a hint of amusement in his voice.

Mohammed snorted. 'I should slit you from throat to belly and watch your thieving guts spill out.'

Emma stepped forward, but she felt Ahmed's hand on her arm, restraining her.

'It would make rather a mess,' the Englishman mused. 'And you'd be the one scrubbing the deck.'

Emma had never seen someone with a sword to their throat before, but she rather thought normally people in fear for their lives didn't joke quite as much.

For a few long seconds Mohammed and the Englishman stared at each other, then they both broke out into wide grins.

'It seems you owe me your life, Oakfield,' Mohammed said as he clapped the dripping Englishman on the back.

'Shall we call it even?'

'You know each other?' Emma asked, feeling the colour rise in her cheeks.

'Alas, it is true. As much as I am loath to

admit it, I have been known to associate with this lowlife,' Oakfield said.

Emma snorted. 'I think it is probably Mohammed who is ashamed to associate with you.'

The Englishman laughed. He stepped forward, closing the distance between them. He took her hand in his own and raised it to his lips.

'Sebastian Oakfield at your service, madame.'

As he lifted his head he looked directly into her eyes and Emma felt something tighten in her stomach. His eyes were a vivid green, a colourful splash against his bronzed skin and sandy blond hair. Emma could see he had tiny lines around his eyes; he was obviously a man who liked to smile a lot.

'Please relinquish the *sitt*'s hand,' Ahmed said, stepping closer.

Sebastian turned to Ahmed as if seeing him for the first time but still did not drop Emma's hand.

'Please forgive my forwardness,' he said, not looking in the least bit repentant. 'But it is not often you get a woman with beauty to rival Nefertiti sailing down the Nile.'

The compliment brought Emma to her senses. She slid her hand from his and took a step back, trying to look unaffected by his honeyed words. She reminded herself she wasn't a young, inexperienced girl any longer. She was a woman of twenty-five. And although she might not have much worldly experience she knew better than to believe the insincere compliments of a rogue. Maybe once…but no longer.

'Step away from my guests, scoundrel,' Mohammed said, swatting Sebastian on the shoulder. 'They don't want to be harassed by the likes of you.'

'Young ladies don't want to be courted by dashing and adventurous gentlemen?' Sebastian said, speaking to Mohammed but his eyes wandering to Emma.

'How do you know this man?' Ahmed asked Mohammed, trying to push his way between the dripping-wet new arrival and Emma.

Emma took a step forward; she didn't want to miss this story.

The glint of humour left Mohammed's eyes and he said seriously, 'I owe my life to Mr Oakfield—without him I would be nothing more than a carcass in the desert.'

Emma glanced at Mr Oakfield, who seemed a little uncomfortable about this revelation. He seemed to be the sort of man who didn't take sincere compliments well, preferring to laugh them off.

'Three years ago, I was attacked by a group of bandits in the desert. They took my money and my clothes and my horse. They left me to try to make my journey on foot—a feat for a man even half my age. Mr Oakfield found me and brought me to safety.' Mohammed paused, as if there was more to the story. 'And he helped me to track down the bandits, who are now languishing in Cairo's most grim prison.'

Mohammed smiled quickly, then turned back to take control of his flotilla. Emma was just about to say something when a shout from the bank of the Nile made everyone turn to look. The six men in white billowing robes had now reached the water's edge and were gesticulating angrily in their direction. None of them, however, seemed prepared to get wet.

'What have you done, Mr Oakfield?' Emma asked, her curiosity finally getting the better of her. He must have done something extremely reckless to be chased by six very angry-looking men with swords.

'You mean apart from losing my heart to the most enchanting woman north of the Equator?'

'You've just met me, Mr Oakfield. I hope

you're not one of those foolish men who believes in love at first sight.'

'Foolish, lovesick…'

Emma heard herself snort again. Mr Oakfield didn't seem to bring out her most ladylike side.

'Did you knock your head when you dived into the Nile?'

He looked as though he was about to deny it.

'I sincerely hope you did,' she murmured.

'May we start again?' Sebastian asked.

Emma gave a gracious nod.

'Sebastian Oakfield, at your service, madame.'

'And tell me, Mr Oakfield, what made you risk life and limb diving into one of the most dangerous rivers in the world?'

Sebastian grinned at her and Emma found her disapproving facade waver. He was a very good-looking man. With an infectious smile. A disarmingly infectious smile.

'I'm so glad you asked, Miss…?'

'Knight. Emma Knight.'

'Miss Knight,' he repeated, his voice low, and Emma knew immediately it was the voice he used with his lovers. A shiver ran down her spine despite the warmth of the late afternoon sun. 'Would you like to see something spectacular?'

Emma allowed him to take her by the hand and lead her over to the scattered cushions she had been sitting on before he'd boarded the felucca. He sat down and gestured for her to sit beside him. Ignoring Ahmed's tut of disapproval, Emma sank into the cushions. She found she was holding her breath as Sebastian reached into the bag he had over his shoulder and pulled out an object that fitted neatly in the palm of his hand.

'Here,' he said, placing the heavy stone object in her hand.

Emma turned it over in her palm and studied it carefully. It was beautiful. It was made of a rock that she didn't recognise, the stone a dark grey in colour, and it was carved into a figure of a man. The features were still visible on his face and the details of his elaborate headdress were obvious even after all these years.

'It's a—'

'Shabti,' Emma interrupted.

Sebastian looked at her appraisingly.

'Late third-century BC, if I'm not mistaken. If I had to hazard a guess, I would say it was from the tomb of a very wealthy man.'

Emma glanced at Sebastian. He was momentarily lost for words. Emma didn't think it was an occurrence that happened often.

'How do you know that?' he asked.

Emma shrugged. 'I've studied a little around the subject.'

That was an understatement. Egyptology had once been a hobby for her, but in the last few years it had become more of an escape. When all else had seemed bleak, Egyptology had been her saviour.

'How did you come by this piece?' Emma asked.

Sebastian studied her for a second, as if contemplating whether to tell her the truth.

'It was just lying around,' he said with a shrug.

Emma felt acute disappointment. She'd wanted him to be honest with her, no matter how unpalatable the truth. She'd had enough lies from men to last her a lifetime. Here was just another man who lied rather than admit the truth. When they reached Cairo she would put him from her mind, even if she struggled to forget the thrill she experienced when he looked at her and smiled.

Chapter Two

Sebastian leaned in closer to the delectable Miss Knight, raised a hand and tucked a stray strand of hair behind her ear. He felt her stiffen at the contact and shift farther away from him. He frowned. If Sebastian was good at anything in life, it was reading other people's expressions and mannerisms. A few minutes earlier, when he had first introduced himself, he'd detected a spark of desire in Miss Knight's eyes. Now she was positively frosty. He wondered exactly what he'd done to bring about this change.

'It's a well-preserved piece,' Emma said, tracing her thumb over the Shabti in her hand. 'I'm sure it's worth a lot of money.'

A good few hundred pounds. Enough to keep him in business for months to come.

'And such historical value. It's a shame, really,' she mused.

'A shame?'

'That it will end up on the bottom of the Nile.'

With a swift movement she leant over the edge of the felucca and held the Shabti above the water.

He lunged forward, catching her wrist in his hand. Her fingers still gripped the artefact but it would only take one movement to send it to the bottom of the river, never to be seen again.

'I don't like being lied to,' she said.

Sebastian almost laughed. She was doing this because he'd lied to her?

'How did you come to be in possession of such a piece?'

He shifted slightly, aware his body was pressed up against hers in a most delightful manner. If he wasn't careful, her protective old bodyguard would have a sword up against his throat for bad behaviour.

'I had a scroll,' he said. 'It hinted at the location of a chamber under the Temple of Horus.'

He saw the interest flash in her eyes and he relaxed. Here was a woman who loved Egypt. She wouldn't destroy a piece of its history by dropping it into the Nile.

'I spent a week searching for it and today I got lucky.'

'And the men who were chasing you?' she asked.

He shrugged. 'They'd noticed my sustained interest in the temple and were out to take the Shabti for themselves. The market for genuine ancient Egyptian artefacts is one where demand is greater than supply. No doubt they worked for one of the more underhand antiquities dealers in Cairo.'

'Was there anything else in the chamber?'

He could hear the excitement in her voice and found her excitement enthusing him. He let go of her wrist and leant back, relaxing.

'The entrance was hidden under a huge stone slab. Once I managed to move it to one side, it revealed a narrow staircase.'

He watched as Emma unconsciously brought her hand back over the side of the boat and cradled the artefact between her fingers. Her eyes were alight with a passion he knew was reflected in his own when talking about archaeology.

'I had to take a flaming torch down the stairs to illuminate the chamber below. The flickering light revealed the most wonderful paintings all over the walls.'

'Were they colourful?' Emma asked.

He nodded.

She looked back towards the Temple of Horus wistfully.

'All the paintings I've seen whilst I've been in Egypt have been exposed to the elements,' she explained. 'The colours have faded. I'd love to see something so well preserved.'

Seb nearly found himself promising to take her to see the chamber below the Temple of Horus, but thankfully stopped himself before the words formed on his lips. The last thing he needed was to spend time acting as tour guide for a wide-eyed English lady. She might be a very pretty lady, but she was off-limits. She had that air of the upper class about her, and, although Seb had left the English gentleman part of his persona behind many years ago when he'd left England, he knew better than to dally with an unmarried innocent young woman. As much as he wanted to.

Emma Knight was exactly the kind of young woman his father had been so eager for him to marry all those years ago. Petite, blonde, pretty and innocent. The very embodiment of the saying 'an English rose'. Seb had refused then, and now he was too old and worldly-wise to get himself in trouble over a pretty face and an enthusiastic smile.

'I would offer to take you to the chamber,' Seb said smoothly, 'but unfortunately I'm not sure I'd be welcome.'

She nodded, clearly disappointed to have missed such a well-preserved slice of Egypt.

'The chamber had a few statues dotted around, and on a raised stone platform was that Shabti.'

Emma glanced down to the Shabti in her hands, running her fingers over the engravings one last time before holding it out to him.

'Thank you,' he said, slipping the artefact back into his bag.

'Will you sell it?' Emma asked.

He nodded.

'I would find it so hard to part with something so beautiful.'

Seb shrugged. Once, many years ago, he'd felt the same, but he couldn't afford to be sentimental now. He had a business to run, and employees who relied on him to sell the artefacts they found, not become attached to them.

Mohammed shouted from the front of the boat and pointed ahead of them.

'Cairo,' Seb explained. 'Is it your first visit?'

Emma nodded, her eyes widening with excitement.

'You won't want to miss this.'

Seb stood and held out his hand to help Emma rise to her feet. They moved to the edge of the felucca and watched the city take shape before their eyes.

Ten years ago when Seb had left England he'd been directionless, moving from place to place. He hadn't known where he would settle or how he would make a living. He'd sailed down the Nile in a felucca very much like this one and when he'd caught his first glimpse of Cairo he'd known he was home.

'It's beautiful,' Emma said.

Seb had heard Cairo being called many things but beautiful wasn't the usual response. Most people fresh from the rolling green hills of England thought Cairo was dirty and dusty. Only a few saw the gem nestled in the desert, the charm of the whitewashed buildings and the narrow streets.

'This is only the beginning,' he said quietly to Emma.

She turned to him, the enthusiasm evident on her face.

'I want to see it all,' she said. 'I can't believe I'm actually here.'

Seb watched her as she looked out at the dusty city. He wondered what this well-brought-up young lady was doing so far away from home. There were plenty of Europeans in Cairo—the West had become interested in what Egypt had to offer in the last few years—but you didn't see many unmarried, basically unchaperoned young women out here on their own.

He glanced at Emma's elderly protector. He was originally from Egypt, if Seb wasn't much mistaken. He watched his young mistress like a hawk, but Seb doubted he would be much use if she actually got herself into a dangerous situation. And he didn't think Miss Emma Knight was the retiring kind of woman who kept herself out of danger well.

'What are your plans when we reach Cairo?' Seb asked.

For the first time since he'd met her, Seb noticed a veil come down over Emma's expression. She glanced at him warily.

'We will be staying with Colonel and Mrs Fitzgerald,' she said after a few seconds. 'They were friends of my father and have promised to help me arrange some trips to see different temples and tombs.'

Intriguing. If he wasn't much mistaken she had a hidden agenda, something she didn't want him to know about.

'Mrs Fitzgerald is at the centre of the Cairo social scene.'

Emma looked at him quizzically. 'There's a Cairo social scene?'

He laughed. 'Nothing like what you'd be used to in London, I'm sure.'

'Are you part of this social scene?'

Seb glanced at her again. Anyone else with that question he would have assumed was flirting with him, but Emma's face was free from guile. She was just genuinely interested.

'The runaway son of an English lord? I'm the guest of honour at most of these events. The community here does love a little bit of scandal.'

He saw her face fall as he said the word scandal and wondered if Emma was running from something back home, too. He couldn't imagine the woman in front of him being embroiled in anything worth gossiping about. She was too open, too sweet in nature.

He didn't have time to enquire further. Mohammed shouted a request and immediately

Seb was on his feet, helping his old friend guide the felucca into the jetty.

Seb breathed in the smell of the city. He felt at home in Cairo. He loved going on trips around Egypt, searching for lost temples or tombs, seeking the pharaohs' treasures of old, but he felt most happy in Cairo.

Once the felucca was secured Seb waited whilst Ahmed and Emma got ready to disembark.

'There's a bit of a gap,' he said. 'Watch you don't fall.'

Emma gathered her skirts in her hand and lifted her foot to step over the side of the felucca. Seb could see she was going to trip before her foot even met the wood. She stumbled, careening towards the water. Instinctively he leant forward and swept her into his arms. He lifted her over the side of the boat and set her gently down on the wooden jetty. Her body was pressed against his and he could feel she was trembling slightly. She looked up at him, her blue eyes sparkling in the sun, and her lips parted a little.

Seb felt his head dip towards hers slowly. One arm was looped around her waist, holding her close to him. The other hand reached up, brushed a strand of hair from her forehead and tucked it behind her ear. It was an intimate act, and Seb could feel Emma's body responding to him. In that instant she wanted to be kissed. And he wanted to kiss her. But he wasn't stupid enough to act on his urges.

Reluctantly Seb released her. Emma's head dipped low, her eyes refusing to meet his, and he saw the first tint of a blush colouring her cheeks.

'Thank you for catching me,' she said, looking up at him again.

Seb swallowed. She was everything he couldn't have, and right now she was everything he wanted.

Chapter Three

'It's far too dangerous for a gently bred young woman to be gallivanting off into the wilds of Egypt without a proper escort,' Mrs Fitzgerald said. There were murmurs of agreement from the other guests around the table.

'I wouldn't be on my own, I'd have Ahmed with me,' Emma protested.

'Still, it's not right. If I allowed you to risk yourself in such a way, your dear papa would never forgive me.'

Emma resisted the urge to point out her dear papa was dead. And that he'd spent most of his youth dragging her mother from camp to camp to study this or that new Egyptian discovery.

'Really you'd be much better to stay in Cairo with us,' Mrs Fitzgerald said. 'We can help arrange for you to have a tour of the new Museum of Antiquities. And you can get up close to the pyramids.'

Emma nodded and tried to look enthusiastic. She was sure Cairo had a lot to offer her. She had been staring at paintings of the pyramids for years, dreaming of the day she'd see them for herself, but this was her adventure and she wasn't going to let Mrs Fitzgerald stand in her way of seeing the more inaccessible parts of Egypt.

'Don't you agree, dear?' Mrs Fitzgerald turned to her husband, who was sitting quietly next to Emma.

'Yes, of course,' he said, not looking up from his plate. 'Far too dangerous.'

Mrs Fitzgerald nodded triumphantly and promptly changed the subject.

'I'll put you in touch with just the chap to be your guide,' Colonel Fitzgerald said to Emma quietly. She glanced at him but he hadn't moved at all. She suspected his wife would not forgive him for going against her advice.

'Thank you,' Emma whispered.

'So how long are you out here, Miss Knight?' a portly older gentleman Emma thought might have been called Sir Henry asked her.

'At least a couple of months,' she said. 'My

father talked of Egypt and Cairo incessantly when I was young. Now that he's gone, I want to experience everything he told me about.'

'Shame a young girl like you hasn't got a husband to take her around the sights,' Sir Henry said, wiggling his eyebrows in a way Emma suspected he thought was suggestive.

She tried not to bristle and reminded herself to keep calm. She was twenty-five, past marriageable age in the eyes of the social circles she moved in. A few years ago comments like Sir Henry's would have hurt her, made her feel inadequate, but Emma had become hardened to them now. She knew she would never marry, never have the family she had once craved. Now she just let the comments and questions wash over her, and tried not to be too upset when she mulled them over in her mind later on.

'You might be well away from the first flush of youth, but I'm sure many men would still want you. Especially men of the older variety.'

Now Emma knew he was proposing himself. She looked him over and tried not to grimace. She'd rather be alone. It wasn't that she thought physical appearance was everything. No, she'd rather have a kind heart and charitable spirit over a chiselled jaw and firm muscles any day, but she thought she should be at least a little physically attracted to any potential spouse.

'Miss Knight decided not to marry after *the incident*,' Mrs Fitzgerald said in a loud whisper.

Emma felt the heat start to creep into her face and looked around for some means of escape. It wasn't that she'd decided not to marry, in fact she'd been certain she was going to get married. It was her liar of a fiancé who'd had other plans.

'Ah, yes, such a shame,' Sir Henry said. 'But the right man might overlook that little indiscretion.'

Emma smiled blandly and wondered if she could pretend to faint. Or vomit onto her dinner plate. Anything to get her away from this conversation.

'We've all made mistakes, after all. Let him who is without sin cast the first stone.' Sir Henry leaned in towards Emma and gave her an encouraging smile.

Emma glanced around, trying desperately to find some way to end this conversation. Her father had once warned her people were less subtle in Egypt. They would say things to your face rather than whisper them behind your back. He said it was because the English community out there was so small, so intimate. At the time

Emma had thought it would be refreshing, not to have people whispering about her behind her back, but now she would give anything not to discuss her tainted past with people she'd only met a few hours before.

'Would you do me the honour of dancing with me?' Colonel Fitzgerald asked suddenly.

Emma could have hugged him.

'But we haven't yet had dessert,' his wife protested.

'I'm sure dessert will be waiting for us when we return,' the colonel said.

He rose and offered his hand to Emma.

'But your heart…' Mrs Fitzgerald said.

'Nothing wrong with my heart.'

Emma stood and allowed the elderly colonel to lead her onto the dance floor.

'Thank you,' she said quietly as they joined the four other couples moving slowly across the floor.

The colonel nodded gruffly. 'They'll have moved on by the time we sit back down.'

He was right. When the dance was over Emma returned to her place at the table and was pleased to find conversation had turned to a dig a few miles outside Cairo.

'There's rumour it could be the big one itself. Rameses.'

There was a moment of silence around the table as everyone considered what a celebration there would be if Rameses' tomb was uncovered.

The conversation continued and Emma turned towards Colonel Fitzgerald and listened to him discussing the fake artefacts flooding the market and deceiving well-intentioned amateur collectors back in England. As he spoke Emma glanced towards the door and felt her heart jump in her chest. Striding through the wide doorway, looking as though he'd just been blown in from the desert, was Sebastian Oakfield.

He caught her staring at him and winked, making the blood rush to Emma's cheeks. She forced herself not to look away or bury her head as she wanted to, but instead gave a nod of acknowledgement before slowly turning back to the colonel.

She didn't know why he affected her in such a way. They'd met only briefly. She couldn't deny he was charming, but the fact that he was a practised charmer should have had her running for the hills even if nothing else did.

Emma risked another glance over her shoulder and almost fell off her chair as she realised he was making a beeline for their table.

'Miss Knight,' he said, his voice low and seductive. 'What a pleasure to see you again.'

He turned his smile on the rest of the company and Emma felt momentarily bereft. She shook her head, trying to find the sense that had abandoned her just seconds before.

'Ladies, what a pleasure. So many beautiful women my eyes don't know where to look.'

The ladies around the table tittered and giggled, and Emma would have sworn Mrs Fitzgerald even batted her eyelashes at the much younger man.

'Colonel Fitzgerald, Sir Henry.' The two men rose and they all shook hands.

'Why don't you come and join our little party?' Mrs Fitzgerald suggested.

Emma stared resolutely at her hands. She wished he wouldn't join them; she found it hard to keep hold of her normally robust common sense when he was around.

'I wouldn't like to intrude…'

'Nonsense, we'd love for you to join us.'

Not needing any more encouragement, Sebastian grabbed a chair from an empty table and placed it next to Emma's, forcing Sir Henry farther away.

'You never mentioned you'd already met Mr Oakfield,' Mrs Fitzgerald said to Emma.

Sebastian turned to her with a look of shock on his face.

'You didn't mention our recent adventure together?'

'Adventure?' Mrs Fitzgerald queried, her voice rising an octave.

Emma shot Sebastian a warning look.

'A most exhilarating adventure,' Sebastian confirmed.

Emma groaned. There was no way Mrs Fitzgerald was going to let her out of her sight after this.

'There I was, minding my own business on the banks of the Nile up near the Temple of Horus.'

Emma rolled her eyes involuntarily.

'Actually, would you like to tell the story, Miss Knight?' Sebastian asked, motioning for her to continue where he'd left off.

'I'm not sure I know how it goes,' Emma said.

Sebastian grinned at her and continued, 'Well, there I was, minding my own business when I hear a shout and before I know it I'm being chased by forty heavily armed Egyptian bandits.'

Emma felt her breath rush through her lips in disbelief. She fought to keep the smile from her face. It would only encourage him.

'Are you sure it was only forty, Mr Oakfield?' Emma asked.

Sebastian cocked his head to one side and pretended to consider. 'Perhaps you're right and it was closer to fifty.' He shrugged. 'It doesn't matter. Forty, fifty, four hundred, however many. The end result was a lot of bandits and only one of me.'

Emma glanced around the table. He had them all enthralled.

'I looked to my left and I looked to my right but there was nowhere to escape. I thought my time had finally come to meet the angels in heaven.'

Emma knew she wasn't the only one who raised her eyebrows at the idea of Sebastian Oakfield going to heaven.

'Then, across fifty feet of fast-flowing Nile water, my eyes met those of a heavenly creature and I knew I was saved. I dived into the water and swam until my lungs were about to burst.

When I surfaced, Miss Knight encouraged me aboard her felucca.'

Emma remembered it rather differently, but she had to admit Sebastian had a certain way with words.

'But I wasn't out of danger yet. The dastardly felucca captain threatened to disembowel me before I could catch my breath. Certain I was about to die, I closed my eyes and waited for the inevitable, but instead I was surprised to find Miss Knight throwing herself in front of the captain's sword for me.'

Mrs Fitzgerald gasped and Emma groaned quietly. She doubted she'd be allowed to leave her room, let alone Cairo, for the duration of her stay.

'Miss Knight persuaded the piratical captain to spare my life and deliver me safely to Cairo. I shall be in her debt for ever.'

He turned his attention back to Emma and took her hand, planting a kiss just below her knuckles. His lips were soft against her skin and for a moment Emma felt as if they were the only two in the room. She forgot all the trouble he'd caused her and the curious stares of the Fitzgeralds and their friends. In that moment she was only aware of her heart thumping in her chest, his lips against her skin, and the primal urge that surged up through her, willing him to pull her against him and claim her as his own.

He released her hand and Emma came tumbling back to reality. She smiled at him shakily, wondering whether he had felt the same thrum of desire as she had. She shook her head; of course he hadn't. He was a man of the world, a charmer—he probably took a different woman to his bed every night. A man like Sebastian Oakfield wouldn't be affected by a mere kiss on the hand, especially not with an inexperienced woman like herself.

'Interesting,' he murmured.

Chapter Four

'Would you give me the pleasure of this dance, Miss Knight?' Sebastian asked as the music swelled in the background.

Emma looked at him for a couple of long seconds before replying and for an instant he thought she might refuse.

'Of course,' she said and delicately got to her feet.

He led her to the dance floor, using the few seconds it took for them to weave around the tables of the other guests to analyse what had just happened. He'd been joking around, as he always did. He'd seen first a flicker of disapproval in Emma's eyes, but soon that had transformed to amusement. Then he'd taken her hand in his and brushed his lips against her skin. Kissing a lady's hand was something he'd done plenty of times, but never before had he felt the same jolt as he had this time, as his lips had met her skin.

Seb glanced about the room. There were plenty of pretty women dotted here and there, many of whom were giving him encouraging smiles. He'd kissed pretty women before, but he'd never felt like this.

Emma reached the dance floor and waited at the edge for him to escort her onto it. He offered her his arm and felt a thrill of pleasure as she slipped her small hand into the crook of his elbow.

She was attractive, Seb couldn't deny it. Her dazzling blue eyes would hold any man's attention and her lips were full and pink and just begging to be kissed. Seb cleared his throat quietly and told himself to behave. Yes, Miss Emma Knight was pretty, but the only reason she was affecting him this way was because he knew he couldn't have her. He'd felt the same when the Egyptian authorities had denied him access to the tombs in the Valley of the Kings. Well, almost.

Glancing at Emma now, he wondered whether he would give up the chance to discover a hundred royal tombs for just one night in her arms.

He grinned. He'd always been prone to fits of romanticism.

'I didn't expect to see you again so soon,' Emma said, clearly trying to make polite conversation as she'd been brought up to do.

'I followed you here,' Seb said bluntly.

He tried to keep a straight face as Emma's expression turned to one of horror.

'You followed me?' she asked.

'Yes, trailed you from the moment we left the dock.'

She frowned warily. 'So you saw where I went this afternoon?'

He nodded vaguely.

'You won't tell the Fitzgeralds I visited the museum without them?'

'Wouldn't dream of it. Your secret's safe with me.'

She looked at him appraisingly for a few seconds then grunted, as if satisfied.

'You didn't visit the museum, did you?' he asked slowly.

'And you didn't follow me, did you?'

Seb grinned again. It wasn't often he came up against anyone who gave as good as they got.

'I didn't follow you,' he admitted in a low whisper. He felt her shiver as he leaned in closer and his breath tickled her ear. 'I didn't have to. It's common knowledge the Fitzgeralds dine at Harcourt's every Thursday. I knew exactly where to find you.'

She looked at him, clearly wondering whether to believe this version of events.

'And I suppose you came specially to see me?'

'Would you believe me if I said I couldn't get you out of my mind?' Seb asked.

Emma laughed.

'You dash all the romance from a fellow,' he grumbled, pretending to be dejected.

The truth was he *had* come to Harcourt's to see her again. Seb had spent the entire afternoon feeling out of control, and if there was one thing he hated it was not being in control. Every time he sat down to translate a document or tally his accounts he would see Emma's face, the expression of awe as she was enthralled by his description of the Temple of Horus. He kept remembering the way she had felt in his arms and kept imagining the taste of her lips. He regretted not kissing her, not brushing his lips against hers just the once so he could relive the experience at his leisure.

He glanced down at those lips now. They

were pursed slightly, as if she were mildly displeased. Emma was frowning, but the twinkle in her eye told Seb that she was only pretending to disapprove.

He spun her in time to the music, marvelling at how easily she kept up. She intrigued him, this petite blonde beauty. He couldn't understand how she'd ended up in Egypt all on her own. She was pretty, accomplished at dancing, quick-witted. She should have had men clamouring for her hand in marriage. But instead here she was, past the age when most young women had settled down, in a foreign country thousands of miles away from home.

'I came tonight because I had to know the answer to a question that's been plaguing me all afternoon,' Seb said.

Emma cocked her head to one side and waited for him to continue.

'Why have you come to Egypt?'

The shutters came down again and Emma looked at him warily. It was Seb's turn to smile encouragingly. He held his breath, not knowing why her answer mattered so much to him.

'My father,' she said. 'He passed away recently. He was an eminent Egyptologist. When I was young he would tell me the most wonderful stories about Egypt. And now…' She trailed off.

Seb understood. She was trying to relive those memories, get closer to her father.

'Most young women wouldn't be brave enough to come to a foreign country on their own.'

She shrugged. 'My father is dead, I don't have any close relatives and I'm unlikely ever to get married. The only way I could make the trip was alone.'

Seb pulled her in closer. Unlikely ever to get married? He wondered why. There was nothing wrong with Emma that he could see. In fact he knew men who would give half their fortunes to marry a pretty and accomplished woman. She was becoming more and more intriguing.

Silently he reminded himself not to pry. He knew the value of privacy. When he'd first arrived in Cairo all those years ago, society had been almost obsessed with his reasons for leaving England. It was common knowledge that he and his father had fallen out, but over the years Seb had managed to keep the rest of the details a secret. If Emma wanted to keep her reasons for visiting Egypt close to her chest, then he wouldn't be the one to pry them from her.

The music stopped and for a few seconds they stood completely still, locked in each other's arms. Seb could feel the rise and fall of Emma's chest against him and he knew she wasn't breathless from the dance. Her lips were a rosy pink and her eyes sparkled in the light. For a moment Seb wanted to sweep her into his arms and carry her off into the night, exploring her body and getting into the closed-off crannies of her mind.

Then reluctantly Emma pulled away and the spell was broken.

'Thank you for a lovely dance, Mr Oakfield,' she said.

Seb forced himself to smile nonchalantly, not wanting her to see how much she had affected him.

'Would you care for a breath of fresh air?' Seb asked, knowing he was playing with fire.

She regarded him silently for a few seconds, then nodded.

He escorted her outside onto the large terrace. They weren't alone, which Seb knew he should be grateful for. Emma incited something inside him that he knew he had to be careful of. The last thing he needed was to be caught in a compromising situation with the very proper Miss Knight.

They made their way over to the stone balustrade and Seb watched as Emma rested her elbows on the cool surface and gazed out into the darkness. His eyes wandered over the delicate curve of her jaw up to her rosy pink lips and he felt the first stirrings of desire. His instinct was to pull her into his arms and kiss her, claim her as his own. He almost laughed at the intensity of his feelings.

He dipped his fingers into his pocket and ran the tips over the rugged surface of the Shabti he'd shown to Emma earlier. For a moment he wondered if bringing it here tonight had been a stupid idea.

'I have a present for you,' he said, watching as her expression turned to one of intrigue.

Slowly he withdrew the Shabti from his pocket and handed it over.

Emma took the carved stone in her hand and turned it over a couple of times.

'I couldn't possibly accept this,' she said, but her eyes gave away her longing for the artefact.

'I want you to have it.'

'But you barely know me.'

It was true, but earlier in the day as they'd sat

side by side in the felucca, Seb had seen a passion in Emma's eyes that he recognised from his own. Owning this Shabti would mean so much to her, and for some reason Seb found himself wanting to make her happy.

'I can't accept this,' Emma repeated, holding out the artefact.

Seb didn't move a muscle, just looked deep into her eyes and smiled.

'It would make me happy if you would accept this as a welcoming gift from the country I love so much.'

Emma drew back her hand and once again studied the Shabti. Eventually she gave a slight nod.

'I will treasure it always.'

Seb knew she spoke the truth.

'Why are you in Egypt, Mr Oakfield?' Emma asked suddenly, turning to face him.

Seb grinned, trying to hide the fact that he'd been staring at her lips and fantasising about pulling her up against him.

He supposed her question was fair. He'd asked her what had brought her to Egypt and she'd answered. Now it was his turn to divulge.

He stepped closer. There was still a good foot

between their bodies, but he could almost imagine how she would feel in his arms.

'Why do you think I came to Egypt, Miss Knight?' he asked, his voice low and seductive.

He saw her swallow, the tiny muscles of her throat contracting in unison as she looked up at him. Then her tongue darted out to moisten her lips and Seb almost groaned. She was enticing, this outwardly prim young woman, and he would bet his year's income she didn't know it.

'I...' she started, her voice barely more than a whisper, then she seemed to compose herself. 'I think you came here for the same reasons I did, Mr Oakfield.'

He cocked an eyebrow.

'For the excitement and the mystery and the quest for knowledge of a civilisation past.'

'Then you think we are alike?' he asked, narrowing the gap between them.

She nodded, her eyes not leaving his.

Seb couldn't help himself. He had to kiss her. Just the once. He couldn't stop himself.

He dipped his head so their lips were inches apart and watched Emma's face. Her lips parted ever so slightly when she realised his intention and her breathing became shallow. Her eyes widened, but she didn't pull away. If anything she swayed slightly towards him.

'I just need to taste you,' Seb murmured. 'Just this once.'

If she'd protested, he would have pulled away. If she'd even looked a little unsure, he would have stopped himself, but if anything she inched even closer to him. In that instant she wanted to be kissed as much as he wanted to kiss her. Tomorrow morning she might regret it—hell, tomorrow morning he might regret it—but right now he knew he had to kiss her.

His lips brushed gently against hers, the touch feather-light. He felt her shudder under his touch and he lightly cupped the back of her head and pulled her closer to him. Emma's lips parted slightly as Seb deepened the kiss and he dipped his tongue gently into her mouth. She groaned with pleasure and the sound went straight to the core of him.

Seb knew he had to stop. He was kissing a woman he barely knew only a few feet from the gossipmongers of Cairo. With one final brush of the lips he pulled away.

Emma looked even more desirable than before. Her cheeks were tinged pink and her hair had a slightly ruffled appearance.

Glancing over his shoulder to check they hadn't been observed, Seb took a moment to compose himself. The kiss had meant to satiate his desire for the delectable Miss Emma Knight; instead it had stoked the flames. Now he wanted nothing more than to throw her over his shoulder and take her to his bed.

'I should apologise,' he said after a few seconds, 'But I fear it would be insincere.'

Emma looked at him as though she were still trying to process what had just happened.

'I can't apologise for something I don't regret,' he said.

Suddenly she shook her head, and looked at him as if she were waking from a dream. Her expression went from one of contentment to one of horror. Lifting a hand to her mouth, she started to back away from him.

'No, no, no, no, no,' she was murmuring.

Seb frowned. He'd kissed plenty of women before and not a single one had responded with abject horror.

'It's all right,' he said soothingly. 'No one saw.'

She shook her head as if he didn't understand.

'How could I be so stupid?' she whispered.

Seb kept quiet; he assumed she was talking more to herself now than to him.

Emma took a couple of deep breaths and closed her eyes for a few seconds. When she re-opened them there was a steely focus about her.

'That was a mistake, Mr Oakfield,' Emma said in a tone that invited no argument. 'I would appreciate it if you would leave. I will make your excuses to the Fitzgeralds.'

Seb knew there was no point arguing. The intimacy they'd shared during the kiss had been shattered, and Emma was not going to allow him another opportunity to relive it.

'Thank you for a lovely evening,' Seb said quietly, taking her hand in his own and raising it to his lips. He felt a thrill of triumph when she didn't pull away, but didn't push his luck any further.

'Goodbye, Mr Oakfield,' Emma said with finality.

Chapter Five

Emma hadn't slept. No, that was a lie; she felt as if she hadn't slept. She'd lain awake for hours tossing and turning, trying to banish Sebastian Oakfield from her mind. Then when she'd finally fallen into a fitful slumber, she'd dreamt about the annoyingly charming man. This morning she felt frustrated and unrefreshed.

She couldn't believe she'd let him kiss her. She grimaced and silently corrected herself—she couldn't believe she had kissed him. There was no point denying that she had been an active participant in the kiss. The worst part was that she'd enjoyed it, and she knew if he'd pulled her into a darkened corner and furthered the embrace she would probably have let him, she'd been so caught up in the moment.

Groaning, Emma buried her face in the pillow. She wished she could erase the past twenty-four hours—then she wouldn't have ever met Sebastian Oakfield, and she would never have kissed him. Or spent the entire night reliving that kiss.

With an effort Emma threw back the light sheet that covered her bed and crossed over to the window. She looked out over the rooftops of Cairo and her mood lifted slightly. Yes, she might have done the exact thing she'd promised herself she'd never do again last night, but this morning she was waking up in Egypt, the land she'd dreamed about for so long.

Emma rested her elbows on the window sill and watched the hustle and bustle of the street below. Men were pushing carts of produce and women were carrying baskets. She wondered if they were headed to the famous Cairo market. Emma yearned to be down there with them, to follow them through the windy streets and explore this exotic city. Momentarily she wished she were a man. Then she'd be free to wander the streets at her leisure, not waiting for a suitable escort and chaperone to take her to only the appropriate sights for a well-brought-up young lady to see. She wanted adventure and freedom, not to have exchanged the constraints of English society for those of an expatriate in Cairo.

A light tap on the door made Emma spin around and she smiled as the young Egyptian maid called Dalila entered the room.

'Would you like to get dressed, miss?' the young woman asked in accented English.

Emma nodded, knowing the hour was already late and she shouldn't waste any more of the day shut away in her room, ruminating over the events of the previous night.

'Were you born in Cairo?' Emma asked Dalila as she slipped the dress over her head.

The young maid nodded. 'I've never left Cairo, miss.'

'What do you think I should see?' Emma asked. 'I know the pyramids and the new Museum of Antiquities, but, as someone who's grown up in Cairo, where do you think a visitor should go to get the authentic feel of the place?'

Dalila paused for a moment, considering. 'The market,' she said eventually. 'Not the tourist antiquities market, but the real thing. Where we go to buy our food and spices. You'll see everyone from the poorest beggar to the richest housewife.'

Emma allowed the maid to fasten the back of her dress and cocked her head to one side. She wondered if she could persuade Mrs Fitzgerald to take her to the market. She doubted it, but it was worth a try.

Making her way downstairs, Emma realised the hour was later than she'd first imagined. The Fitzgeralds had both already had breakfast, but the colonel was still sitting at the table, sipping strong, dark coffee.

'Good morning,' he said genially.

Emma liked Colonel Fitzgerald, even after knowing him for only a day. He was a kind old man. The previous night he had saved her from embarrassment by rescuing her from Sir Henry's unwanted advances. And he had offered to introduce her to a guide who would take her into the wilds of Egypt.

'I'm sorry I slept so late,' Emma said, sitting down at the table. 'I must have been tired after the journey.'

'Nonsense,' he said with a wave of his hand. 'You are a guest in our house, you can sleep in until whatever time you like.'

He motioned to a young man who darted from the room and within seconds returned with plates of food balanced on his arms. He set them in front of Emma with a flourish and she inspected each dish in turn.

'We can have the cook make you something more English if you prefer.'

Emma shook her head. Everything looked delicious; she didn't know where to start.

'This here is flat bread, served with a bean, onion and tomato dip. Or if you prefer something sweet, the honey and nut pastries are delicious.'

The Egyptian footman returned with a steaming cup of strong coffee and placed it on the table. Then he melted into the background, allowing Emma to make a start on the feast in front of her.

'What are your plans for today, my dear?' Colonel Fitzgerald asked after a few minutes.

Emma took a sip of coffee before speaking.

'I'm not too sure. Mrs Fitzgerald kindly said she would take me to see the pyramids next week. Possibly the Museum of Antiquities.'

Colonel Fitzgerald nodded in agreement.

'A very interesting place. However, I was thinking we might take advantage of the fact that Mrs Fitzgerald has a charity meeting arranged, so we could organise for that guide to take you deeper into rural Egypt.'

Emma's eyes lit up immediately. She could feel her pulse quicken at the prospect of exploring Egypt properly, with just a guide for company, discovering long-abandoned temples and following in the footsteps of the Ancient Egyptians.

'He might take a bit of persuasion—he can be a stubborn man when he wants to—but I'm sure you'll be able to convince him to be your guide.'

Emma was imagining a weathered old Egyptian who knew every inch of his country.

'And if that doesn't work, you can remind him he owes you his life.'

Emma frowned. She opened her mouth to question Colonel Fitzgerald then promptly closed it again. Sebastian. He was talking about Sebastian Oakfield. The man who had rendered her senseless with just one kiss. There was no way she could spend a week with him. Who knew what would happen?

Silently she admonished herself. She was stronger than that. Granted, she had allowed the man to kiss her on their second meeting, but now she was savvy to his charms. She would recognise the fiery look in his eyes and that seductive smile and she would put a halt to any further kisses.

Emma gave a tiny nod. She might have fallen for Sebastian Oakfield's charm once, but she wouldn't do it again. Her life had already been ruined by one man who had convinced her kissing and intimacy weren't wrong; she wouldn't make the same mistake.

'We must make sure Mrs Fitzgerald doesn't get wind of your plans. She'll crucify us both if she thinks I've let you go off unchaperoned into the desert.'

Emma felt herself smile weakly. Maybe Mrs Fitzgerald would have a point.

'Of course I wouldn't let you go off gallivanting with anyone. I know Mr Oakfield would do anything to protect your virtue. He's a good man.'

Emma wanted to ask the colonel to expand on this information but didn't want to seem too keen.

'He's helped me out of one or two scrapes myself,' Colonel Fitzgerald continued. He lowered his voice before saying more. 'There was one mission for the army Oakfield assisted us with. A group of bandits had kidnapped the daughter of a very important visitor. Oakfield guided us to their camp in the desert and rescued the girl himself. He's a handy man to have around in a crisis.'

Emma sensed there was more to the story,

some further reason Colonel Fitzgerald trusted Mr Oakfield completely.

'What's more,' the colonel continued, 'the girl became infatuated with him. Kept throwing herself at him. Oakfield didn't bat an eyelid. One of the most trustworthy and upstanding men I know.'

Emma thought about their kiss on the balcony and wondered what Colonel Fitzgerald would make of it.

'He really is the best guide as well,' Colonel Fitzgerald mused. 'Can't think of a single other chap who knows the desert better.'

Emma smiled. If he was the best, then he was the guide for her. Her trip into rural Egypt required someone with good knowledge of the country.

'Then he sounds like just the man.' She paused, wondering if she should continue. In the end her curiosity won out. 'What is it that Mr Oakfield does exactly?' she asked.

The colonel laughed. 'No one really knows. He acquires artefacts, brokers deals, translates scrolls. He's a man with many talents.'

Emma pushed a little further. 'I wonder what brought him to Egypt in the first place,' she mused.

'Some family problem, I think. It's common knowledge he doesn't speak to his father. I think it all started with a falling out around the time of his mother's death. Whatever it was, I'm glad he decided to stop here. He's a good opponent in cards, and a handy man to have around in a crisis.'

A family problem. Bad debts? An illegitimate child? Emma's mind started throwing out hundreds of different possibilities.

Emma sipped the last mouthful of coffee before standing.

'When would be a good time to go and see Mr Oakfield?' she asked.

'I will be ready in half an hour. Shall we meet at noon?'

Emma ascended the stairs to the first floor. Her room was at the end of a short corridor. Just as she rounded the corner she heard a soft thud followed by a scraping sound. She froze, then forced herself to continue. The door to her room was slightly ajar. She was sure she'd left it closed. Shaking her head, she reminded herself that Dalila or one of the other maids could be inside right now, cleaning the room. Nevertheless Emma found that her hands were shaking as she pushed open the door.

A figure clad entirely in black flowing robes froze as she entered the room. Emma gasped in shock, all the breath leaving her body in an instant. She tried to scream but found the muscles in her throat had seized up. Instead of an ear-splitting scream a tiny croak escaped her lips.

Instantly the figure was on his feet. With a final glance around the room he vaulted over the small table and out of the window.

Finally galvanised into action, Emma rushed to the window just in time to see her mysterious intruder disappear around the corner.

In shock, Emma sank onto the bed and felt her hands start to shake. She hadn't managed to get a good look at the intruder—the baggy robes had disguised his build, and all but his dark eyes had been covered on his face—but she knew she'd recognise those eyes if she ever saw them again.

Once she had regained a little of her composure she contemplated calling one of the servants, but quickly dismissed the idea. She knew exactly what the mysterious intruder had been searching for, and luckily she had had the forethought to tuck it into a concealed pocket in her skirt before breakfast. Informing the household of the intruder would just open her up to questions of what he could have been searching for.

Emma's hand closed around the small scroll in her pocket as she reassured herself it was still there. This was her father's most treasured possession, and he had bequeathed it to her on his deathbed. For years he had studied the scroll, making notes on the accompanying pieces of paper, deciphering the ancient language and piecing together a location from the obscure references. Emma had wondered whether he had planned one final trip to Egypt before he died.

Quickly she stood and straightened out the room. The intruder hadn't made much mess—there were just a few papers to be straightened and the sheets on the bed to be smoothed.

After a couple of minutes she looked around the room with satisfaction; no one would know anything untoward had happened here.

Grabbing her parasol and closing the door to her bedroom behind her, Emma realised the incident had made it even more imperative that she find a suitable guide quickly. She didn't want to put the Fitzgeralds in danger. So if that meant begging Mr Oakfield to be her guide, well, she would have to swallow her pride and do just that.

Chapter Six

Seb whistled while he worked. He was in a good mood: he'd found a buyer for his latest acquisition, and today some scrolls he had been waiting for had been delivered to his office. Everything in life was going smoothly.

Well, almost everything. There was the small issue of Miss Emma Knight, the petite Englishwoman who seemed to have bewitched him during their first meeting. Sebastian was a man of the world; he'd flirted and kissed and shared intimate nights with a good number of women. The encounters had always been fun but fleeting. Many years ago he'd realised he would never marry, never have children. It was a choice he had made, and one he made sure the women in his life were well aware of before they became intimate.

Emma was not the sort of woman he should

be dallying with. She was obviously from a re-spectable family, and was the sort a man ought to propose to if he compromised. There was nothing on earth that would convince Seb to get married; he wasn't going to make the same mistakes his parents had.

Therefore the best solution would be to avoid the very alluring Miss Knight so he didn't find himself seducing her on dark terraces and wish-ing for more.

An image of his mother flashed into his mind and he stopped what he was doing momentarily. He missed her. He missed her quiet voice and gentle smiles. Every day he wished he'd been able to persuade her to leave his father, to come away with him and start a new life, free from fear of violence in the one place she should feel safe. Sebastian knew he had failed her, knew her death would always sit heavily on his con-science. Silently he cursed his father, and the image of the man he hated most in the world reminded him why getting involved with any-one like Emma Knight was a bad idea.

There was a sharp rap on the door and Seb jumped a little as he was roused from his thoughts.

'Come in,' he called.

'Colonel Fitzgerald is here to see you,' Tariq, his assistant, announced.

Seb nodded and a couple of seconds later Colonel Fitzgerald entered the room followed by Emma Knight.

Seb tried to suppress a groan. Emma hadn't seemed the type prone to hysterics, or likely to make a scene out of their kiss the night before, but he had only known the woman for one day.

'Colonel, Miss Knight, what an unexpected pleasure.'

The colonel smiled. He didn't look like a man who was about to demand Seb 'do the right thing and marry the girl.' Seb liked the colonel. They'd spent some time working together before the colonel had semi-retired from the army, been on missions that had bonded the two men together as only danger could.

'Please have a seat.' He gestured to the two leather chairs facing his desk and watched as his guests sat down. Once they were comfortable he sent Tariq to make some coffee then took a seat himself.

'What can I do for you today?'

Emma wasn't meeting his eye. In fact she looked more nervous than either of the previous occasions that he'd met her. One hand was twisting the material of her dress whilst the other was tapping out a silent beat on the side of her chair.

'We need a favour,' Colonel Fitzgerald said, getting straight to the point.

Seb raised an eyebrow and felt himself relax inside. So Emma hadn't let the secret of their kiss slip out.

'What sort of favour?'

Colonel Fitzgerald motioned for Emma to speak. Seb watched as she swallowed, straightened her spine then lifted her head to meet his eyes.

Her gaze was unwavering and Seb felt himself shift under her scrutiny.

'Colonel Fitzgerald assures me you are the best,' she said.

Seb couldn't help himself, he grinned. Emma's eyes immediately widened as she realised what she'd just said but she ploughed on.

'The best guide. That you have the best knowledge of Egypt.'

Seb didn't deny it. He had scoured almost every mile of the country at one point or another. The only places in Egypt he hadn't been were the bottom of the Nile and a few of the desert villages.

Tariq knocked quietly at the door and set a

tray of coffee down on the desk. Silently he poured three cups. Just as he was about to leave Colonel Fitzgerald caught his eye.

'Might I have a quick word about the latest shipment?' the colonel asked.

Tariq nodded and waited for Colonel Fitzgerald to follow him from the room.

'Alone again,' Seb murmured.

Emma cleared her throat and ignored his comment.

'I need a good guide, the best, to take me into rural Egypt.'

Seb looked at her for almost a minute. It was a strange request. Certainly he'd acted as a guide for archaeological expeditions before, but never had he had a lone woman ask him to guide her through the wilds of Egypt.

'There are sightseeing trips,' he said. 'Groups of like-minded people who see the main sights Egypt has to offer.'

Emma shook her head. 'I don't want to see the main sights.' She paused and corrected herself. 'At least, I do want to see the main sights, but that's not why I'm here.'

Seb waited for her to continue.

'I have a specific destination in mind.'

'Where?'

'I can't tell you, at least not yet.'

'So you want me to be your guide to a specific destination but you won't tell me where?'

She nodded.

'I would find it rather difficult to guide you if I didn't know where we were going.'

'I would tell you, but only when we had got underway.'

Miss Knight was becoming more and more intriguing.

'Perhaps if you have a map I could indicate a general area,' Emma suggested.

Seb got to his feet and crossed to a set of drawers. He opened one, pulled out a map of Egypt and set it on his desk.

He watched as Emma smoothed down the edges and started to trace the familiar places with her fingertips. Despite her only having arrived in Cairo the day before Seb could tell she loved Egypt. A feather-light smile graced her lips as she ran her finger over Luxor and Alexandria and the great empty space of the desert.

'We would start by heading down towards Luxor,' Emma said.

'The best way to reach Luxor is by boat.'

She shook her head.

'We would need to go via the desert.'

When she didn't elaborate any further Seb placed a finger on Cairo and then traced a route through the desert.

'The desert is harsh and unforgiving. It would take a week to travel from Cairo to Luxor, if you hire good quality horses and have the stamina to stay in the saddle all day.'

'So you'll do it?' Emma asked, her face lighting up.

Seb shook his head. 'I'm sorry, Miss Knight, but I don't take on jobs like this.'

'Jobs like what?'

'Mystery jobs. I need to know what I'm getting myself into.'

Emma sighed and stood. 'I'm sorry to waste your time,' she said. 'Could you recommend anyone else who might be interested?'

Seb felt the blood drain from his face. He knew plenty of reprobates who would jump at the chance of luring a pretty young woman out into the desert.

'The people of Egypt are kind and welcoming,' he said slowly, 'but unfortunately here, as in the rest of the world, there are criminals People who will agree to do something only to abandon you in the middle of the desert with no money and no means of transport.'

Emma's eyes widened, but in indignation, not shock. 'I might look inexperienced and naive, Mr Oakfield, but I can assure you I know what dark streaks can run through people.'

He hoped not. A sheltered young woman shouldn't have to know of the underbelly of society.

'I just urge you to be careful in selecting a guide.'

'I was. I came to you.'

He couldn't argue with her logic.

She stood and started to cross over to the door. Seb could just picture her paying some sleazy man to guide her into the desert, only for him to take advantage of her and leave her for dead.

He ran a hand through his hair. It was none of his business; he hardly knew her. It wasn't his job to protect her. Surely the Fitzgeralds would screen out the most unsuitable of guides.

Cursing silently, he strode over to the door and placed a hand on the wood just as Emma was turning the handle. He hated not being in control, and right now Emma was forcing his hand.

'Why don't you tell me a little more about

your proposed route?' he asked through grit-ted teeth.

The smile she gave him was almost worth it in itself. Seb could feel the tendrils of desire start to creep from somewhere deep inside him and wanted nothing more than to reach out and brush his fingers across her silky cheeks.

Emma broke the spell by bounding back across the room and flopping down into her chair. With a grimace Seb followed.

'I would like to travel down through the des-ert about twenty miles west of the Nile.' She traced her fingers along the map. 'There are a few landmarks we would need to pass before I could tell you the rest of the directions.'

Slowly Seb realised what this was all about. She had a map, or at least a description of a route. That was why she was playing things close to her chest.

He shifted, wondering how to break it to her that most of the maps and scrolls circulating were fakes or forgeries. They promised tombs filled with untold riches, undiscovered since an-cient times. In reality the scrolls had been pro-duced *en masse* by a wily entrepreneur with dubious morals, eager to con an unsuspecting customer.

'Emma,' he started, then quickly corrected himself, 'Miss Knight, it would be extremely difficult to plan a trip without knowing the final destination you had in mind.'

She shook her head as if it were impossible to tell him any more.

'I would at least need to know a few more details. Perhaps you are working off a map or something that you might wish to share with me?'

Again another shake of her head. She wasn't as naive as all that.

'Would you step outside for a minute, Mr Oakfield?' Emma asked.

Trying not to show his amusement at being banished from his own office, Seb graciously stepped outside and closed the door. He'd give her a minute and no more. No doubt she was retrieving the scroll from wherever it was hidden on her person. He closed his eyes and leant his head back against the wall; he could almost picture her rolling up the hem of her skirt, exposing the creamy white skin of her legs.

He groaned softly. Spending two weeks in the desert with Emma would be the worst idea imaginable. Not only would they be going off on a wild goose chase, he would be subjected to two weeks in the company of a woman he found exquisitely alluring.

Rousing himself, Seb pushed open the door with no warning knock. Emma almost jumped from her seat. He heard the rustle of paper or papyrus and caught a glimpse of the scroll she was doing her best to hide away in her skirts.

Seb's breath caught in his throat. He'd only seen one corner of the document, but that was enough to set his heart pounding. The royal seal of Rameses II was in the top left corner. The papyrus was old, almost falling apart and the ink that had been used was faded.

Seb had seen plenty of forgeries that looked this good, but something made him pause. There was a quality about the document, something he couldn't quite put his finger on, that made him certain it was genuine. Miss Emma Knight had somehow got her hands on an authentic Ancient Egyptian scroll.

He tried not to let his excitement show. For years he had been searching for something like this, an opportunity to discover an important tomb for himself. Nonchalantly he strolled over to his desk and sat down.

'Have you any more information for me?'

Seb asked, trying to keep the excitement from his voice.

What he really wanted was a good look at the document. He wondered if it was a map or a written passage, something that described a location.

'From my calculations it would take about a week to reach the destination I have in mind.'

Seb mentally calculated where that would take them on the map. Close to Luxor, close to the tombs in the Valley of the Kings. Over a decade ago Belzoni had discovered a few new tombs in the area, but not much had been uncovered since. Maybe Emma had a map of the location of an undiscovered pharaoh's tomb.

He frowned. If that was the case, he was unsure why they had to go by land. It would take them a few days to travel from Cairo to Luxor on the river, and from there the Valley of the Kings was easily accessible.

So maybe it was somewhere else altogether.

'And who would be travelling?' Seb asked.

'Just myself and Ahmed.'

A small party, then. And notably no female chaperone.

Seb sighed and then nodded. 'Very well, Miss

Knight. I'll do it. But you will have to trust me with more details once the trip is underway.'

Emma bounded from her seat and threw her arms around his neck. Seb was unprepared for her reaction. He felt her lithe body press up against his and instinctively his arms encircled her waist, pulling her in closer to him. She was warm and firm beneath his touch and Seb wanted nothing more than to lay her back on the desk and cover her with his body.

With great self-resolve Seb gently pulled away. He was going to be living in close proximity with Emma for the next couple of weeks, so he would have to learn to curb his urges.

Chapter Seven

Emma fastened her bonnet under her chin and tucked a stray strand of hair behind her ear. The desert was going to be an unforgiving place. Within minutes her skin would redden and freckle, her throat would become parched and she would start to perspire. She knew all of this and more. She knew one wrong turn and they could be lost for weeks amongst the sand dunes, without water or hope of rescue. She knew there could be bandits eager to rob them for any money they carried or even just for a flask of water.

Emma knew of all the dangers but she still couldn't help but feel a thrum of anticipation for the expedition. All her life she had been sheltered, shielded from the real world. And all her life she had listened to her father's stories of Egypt, of the adventures he'd shared with her mother when she was alive. Now here she was, about to set off on an adventure of her own.

'Are you ready, my dear?' Colonel Fitzgerald asked as she hurried down the stairs to the hallway.

Emma glanced behind her, wondering whether she was making a mistake. It would be so easy to call the whole thing off, to spend the next month enjoying civilised Cairo, but she would regret her cowardice for the rest of her life.

'I'm ready.'

Colonel Fitzgerald was taking her to meet Sebastian. Mrs Fitzgerald still had no idea Emma was about to set off into the desert with just Mr Oakfield as her guide. Emma knew it was cowardly, but she was glad she wasn't going to be there when Mrs Fitzgerald found out. No doubt Colonel Fitzgerald would be subjected to a long lecture on how irresponsible he'd been to allow her to go gallivanting off into the desert with no female chaperone. Maybe the old colonel would claim he'd hired someone for the occasion.

Ahmed came hurrying down the stairs carrying her small bag. She had packed light, forgoing all the luxuries she had brought with her to Egypt. She knew they would be riding all day and camping at night. There would be no spare water to bathe in and no spare horses to carry her baggage. She had packed just one change of underclothes and one clean dress, the lightest garment she possessed. The bundle Ahmed carried weighed hardly anything and Emma was confident she would be able to transport it all the way herself if required.

Just as they were about to leave, Dalila came hurrying towards them with a soft bundle over her shoulder.

Colonel Fitzgerald turned to Emma and explained, 'Dalila is going to visit her family for a few days, but if anyone asks she is to be your chaperone whilst you are in the desert.'

Emma nodded, understanding how the colonel's mind worked. He might be happy to trust Sebastian Oakfield with her virtue, but he wasn't silly enough to think other people had the same high opinion of him. This deception would protect her reputation.

Colonel Fitzgerald led their little procession out of the house and up into the carriage. Emma found herself unable to sit still; she was nervous, she realised, and it wasn't entirely because of the nature of the trip. Her mind kept skirting around the real issue that was bothering her, unable or unwilling to admit that she was nervous about spending such a long time in Sebastian's company.

The man did things to her brain she couldn't explain. Ever since that ill-advised night with Freddie, and the disastrous morning after, Emma had built up her defences. The charms of men no longer worked upon her. She could see a lingering look or dazzling smile for what it really was: flirtation with no real meaning. She had continued to socialise, despite all the disgusted looks and whispering behind hands, but she had done so with her defences firmly up.

But Sebastian was another matter altogether. Ever since the first moment their eyes had met over the sparkling waters of the Nile, Emma hadn't been able to get the man out of her head. She seemed to lose all reason when she was around him. A smile or a fleeting touch set her heart pounding in her chest and made her want to smile or touch back. She found herself thinking of him even when he wasn't around, imagining his response to a comment in a conversation, or his smile when something amusing was said.

It was ridiculous, when she thought about it. She'd only met the man three times and now she was imagining him everywhere.

Emma supposed it was inevitable, really. Sebastian was a good-looking man, in an unconventional way. He didn't look or act a single bit like Freddie, or the other men of her acquaintance back in England, and she supposed that was part of his appeal. Whereas most Englishmen would be ashamed of bronzed skin, which showed they spent most of the day outdoors, Sebastian probably rolled his sleeves up at every opportunity. And his shock of blond hair wasn't cut or styled to the latest fashion, it just flopped over his eyes like an unruly mane. His personality, so carefree and happy, was also a contrast to the men of the ton, who seemed to want to pretend they were bored and tired of everything. Sebastian was a man who looked as if he could enjoy himself.

Emma shook her head ruefully. She shouldn't be thinking of him that way. Sebastian Oakfield was her guide, nothing more. She was paying the man to escort her through Egypt. She shouldn't be thinking about his unruly hair or bronzed skin or the way his eyes sparkled in the sunlight like the most precious of jewels.

She was a mature woman, not a girl any longer. Sebastian might be handsome and funny and kind, but any involvement with him other than the strictly professional would be a bad idea, and so she would just have to put his charming smile from her mind.

The carriage slowed to a stop and Emma took a second to compose herself before getting down. She allowed Colonel Fitzgerald to take her hand and assist her to the ground, and had to force herself not to cling to the old man. This was her adventure and she was going to enjoy every second of it.

'Miss Knight.' Sebastian's low voice in her ear made her shiver with anticipation. 'Are you all ready for our expedition?'

The croak that came from Emma's throat made her wish the ground would just open up and swallow her whole. Taking a deep breath, she coughed, then turned to face Sebastian.

'I'm very much looking forward to getting started,' Emma said.

'It's not going to be an easy two weeks,' Sebastian warned as he turned back to one of the beautiful horses and adjusted the harness.

'I'm prepared for that.'

'Most nights we will sleep under the stars.'

Emma tried not to look too excited. She'd always dreamed of sleeping under the stars in the desert, like a true adventuress.

'I am looking forward to falling asleep with nature around me.'

'And it's going to be unbearably hot, in the day.'

'I like the heat.'

'And freezing cold at night.'

'That'll be a nice respite from the warmth of the day.'

'The desert is filled with dangerous creatures and bandits.'

Emma smiled sweetly at Sebastian. 'I'm confident you'll protect me.'

'So you haven't changed your mind?' Sebastian studied her face for a long few seconds.

'I haven't changed my mind,' she confirmed.

Sebastian broke out into a full grin. 'Good, I'm looking forward to the next two weeks.'

He turned away and shouted an order in Arabic. Two boys came scuttling towards them and stood to attention before Sebastian.

'Miss Knight, can I introduce you to our travelling companions? This is Akil and this is Akins.'

The two boys saluted.

'Nice to meet you, missus,' Akil said.

He was nudged hard by his brother who whispered something in his ear.

'Miss,' he corrected himself.

'It is a pleasure to meet you, too.'

The two boys looked almost identical apart from their heights. Emma surmised they were brothers, maybe a year apart in age. Both had a shock of dark hair, round dark eyes and were covered in bruises on their arms and legs. She guessed they were probably a handful.

Sebastian said something else in Arabic and the boys scuttled away, each to a horse who was far too large for their small frames.

'We travel light. It will be just the two of us, the boys and Ahmed.'

Emma swallowed. The next couple of weeks were going to be intimate, to say the least.

'Where's your luggage?' Sebastian asked, turning to look into the carriage.

Emma motioned to the small bundle by her feet.

Sebastian's eyes widened with surprise.

'That's all you've brought?'

Emma nodded.

He picked up the bundle and opened it. Emma started to protest but he silenced her with a stern look.

'I need to make sure you've got what is needed to survive for two weeks in the desert.'

'I packed light,' Emma said quietly as he examined the contents of her bundle.

'Good.' He held up the dress she'd brought. 'It covers up most of your skin. An hour in the desert and you can burn so much your skin blisters.'

Emma felt a small measure of accomplishment that she'd managed to pack the right dress.

Sebastian continued through her bundle, rifling through the contents. Suddenly Emma froze; the only other things she'd packed were her undergarments, which meant Sebastian was now handling them.

She snatched the bundle back and tried to fight the blush she knew was rising to her cheeks. Sebastian didn't look even a little abashed.

'The dress is good,' he said, 'and I'm no expert in whatever women insist on wearing under their dresses, but as long as it's comfortable that's fine. What I don't see is something for the night-time.'

Emma frowned. Surely he didn't expect her to change into a nightgown and slippers to sleep under the stars.

He laughed at her expression. 'Something to keep you warm at night. No matter, I'm sure I've got something that will do.'

He winked at her then turned back to the horse before she could even think of a response.

'This mare will be yours. Her name's Wadjet and she's a little headstrong, but treat her with respect and she'll be the best horse you've ever ridden.'

Emma inched forward and gently placed a hand on Wadjet's neck. She cooed softly and began to stroke the chestnut mare.

'You have ridden before?' Sebastian asked, as if it had only just occurred to him to enquire.

'I've ridden before.'

In truth Emma loved riding. There was something rather liberating about being on a horse. She liked the freedom, the idea that she could just gallop off into the distance and be completely on her own. She'd started riding more since the incident with Freddie, using the pastime as an escape from the unwelcome stares and comments from the rest of her social group.

'There is still time to change your mind,' Sebastian said, moving in closer towards her, closing the distance between them in a single stride.

Emma felt her breathing become shallower, and she struggled to maintain her composure.

She tilted her chin so she was looking up into his eyes and immediately knew that was a mistake. She needed to sever this connection between them, not intensify it.

'I won't think any less of you.'

Emma shook her head. He might not think less of her, but she would. She would never forgive herself for pulling out now.

'I am completely certain I want to go ahead with this expedition,' Emma said, looking Sebastian squarely in the eye.

There was a pause, a couple of seconds where they both remained completely still until Sebastian grinned.

'Good. I've been looking forward to this for days.'

Chapter Eight

Seb finished securing the last few bags and turned to survey the yard. He couldn't count the number of expeditions he'd been on in the last few years. Every few weeks he would set out into the wilderness, sometimes on his own, sometimes accompanied by a few of his most trusted employees. Never before had he taken someone like Emma along with him though.

He wondered if it really was a good idea. She didn't know what she was letting herself in for, that was for sure. He could emphasise the dangers all he liked, but nothing prepared you for your first experience of the desert. The days were scorchingly hot, the nights freezing cold, and the terrain one of the most inhospitable on earth.

He pictured the corner of the scroll he'd caught a glimpse of and knew he needed to go on this expedition. All the time he'd spent in Egypt he'd been waiting for something like this, something big, something to discover for himself. Here was his opportunity. And if it meant taking the delectable Miss Knight along for the ride then he'd just have to remain professional and do what she was employing him to: be her guide.

He glanced over to the entrance of the yard, where there was some commotion. Colonel Fitzgerald had just left, after bidding a fond farewell to Emma, but another small group had arrived. He scrutinised the newcomers with interest. It was possible someone else had got wind of the scroll already and they were coming to threaten or cajole their way onto the expedition.

His frown lifted as Ahmed, Emma's stalwart companion, greeted the three men warmly. He watched as the older Egyptian listened carefully to what was being said, his face crumpling at the news.

After a few minutes Ahmed separated himself from the group and made his way directly to Seb.

'Can I speak with you?' Ahmed asked, his face grave.

Seb lcd the way inside and up to his office. He motioned for Ahmed to have a seat and waited silently for the older man to start to speak.

'I have known Miss Knight since she was a babe in arms,' Ahmed said quietly, 'and her father for even longer. When I was a young man her father saved me from an awful fate, and I have travelled with him ever since.'

'And now you travel with Miss Knight, protecting her.'

Ahmed bowed his head.

'It is my duty and my pleasure.'

Seb remained silent, allowing Ahmed to continue.

'I have just received some saddening news. My father is an old man. He is well into his eighth dccade and his health isn't what it was. I have not seen him for almost twenty-four years.'

Seb nodded sympathetically. He could tell Ahmed cared greatly for his father.

'The men that just arrived—they were my brothers. They have come to tell me our father will not be on this earth much longer. If I ever want to see him again I will have to hurry.'

'Then you must go to your father before it is too late.'

Ahmed nodded, then fixed Seb with a piercing stare.

'Miss Knight is like the daughter I never had. She is the most precious thing in the world to me.'

Seb kept his face impassive.

'Please do not hurt her.'

'I promise,' Seb said simply.

Ahmed looked at him long and hard and finally nodded in satisfaction.

'I have been making enquiries about you, Mr Oakfield,' Ahmed said.

Seb raised an eyebrow.

'You put on a good facade. If you just scratch the surface everyone says you're charming and maybe even slightly frivolous, but that's not the whole truth, is it?'

Seb didn't know how to respond. He knew he had a public persona and a private one. Not that he had to put on a happy demeanour or carefree attitude—he genuinely found life to be pleasurable—it was just he didn't let many people see what was underneath, the serious side to him.

'You are a good man, Mr Oakfield. You run a successful business and you care for your employees. You rescue orphans from the streets and give them respectable jobs. And you've never been involved in a scandal with a woman of good birth.' This last part was said rather pointedly.

Seb shrugged modestly; he was who he was. And he cared for the people around him, be they employees or friends.

'I'm sure you've heard some details of Miss Knight's past,' Ahmed said, lowering his voice even though they couldn't be overheard.

Seb shook his head. He'd assumed there had been some kind of scandal by the way she reacted to certain things, but he hadn't sought out the gossip.

Ahmed sighed and cocked his head to one side, as if contemplating whether he should reveal more.

'I think you should know,' he said. 'Then you'll understand.'

Seb sat back in his chair, wondering what could have happened that was quite so scandalous.

'Miss Knight was always an innocent and impressionable young woman. She saw the best in people, couldn't imagine anyone would be cruel or crafty.'

Seb imagined Emma as a fresh-faced debu-

tante, excited to finally enter the world of the
ton and all the frivolities that accompanied it.

'She was swept up in her season and I think,
having no mother, no one had thought to warn
her of the dangers some of the men posed.'

Seb felt a sudden stab of anger. Someone had
hurt her, and that hurt him. He pushed away
the feeling and tried to concentrate on Ahmed's
narrative.

'She fancied herself in love with a young
man, Freddie Hunter. He insisted they keep
their relationship secret. I think Miss Knight
thought it romantic.'

Seb found he was holding his breath, waiting
to see what the seedy Freddie Hunter had done
to Emma, how he'd hurt her.

'One night he proposed marriage to her, but
refused to let her announce the engagement.'

Seb knew where this story was going and he
felt some of Emma's pain.

'Somehow he persuaded Miss Knight to become intimate with him. They were discovered
and Hunter refused to do the right thing. He left
the country.'

'Emma must have been devastated.'

'She thought she loved him, and he loved
her. For months she hid herself away whilst the

ton gossiped. We thought he'd destroyed her for ever.'

Seb shook his head. 'She's stronger than that.'

'Slowly she started to come out of herself. She realised what kind of man Hunter was and I think accepted she wasn't entirely to blame. Society still gossiped but Miss Knight ignored them. She smiled and danced and reconnected with her old friends.'

'But she never trusted a man again.'

Ahmed shook his head. 'And because of the scandal no one eligible has ever pursued her.'

Seb wondered how the men of the ton could be so stupid. Emma was clearly kind and beautiful. How could they let the unforgivable actions of this Freddie Hunter keep them from seeing how special Emma was?

'That is why I ask you to be gentle with her.'

Seb's head snapped up.

'She is a strong woman, stronger than any other woman I've ever known. She has been through so much and survived. But she is still vulnerable.'

Seb thought back to their kiss on the terrace and wondered if he should feel guilty given everything he knew now.

'I will not be able to accompany you on this

expedition, but I think you will look after her. I would not trust just anyone with her life. I ask that you tread as carefully with her feelings as you do with her safety.'

Seb regarded Ahmed for a minute in silence.

'You have my word.'

The two men shook hands, an understanding passing between them that couldn't be put into words.

Seb led the way back down to the courtyard below and watched as Ahmed approached Emma. He was just out of earshot, but he could imagine the exchange between them, aided by their expressions and gestures. Ahmed quickly told her of his predicament and Seb could see Emma was already urging him to go to be with his family. She wasn't in the least bit selfish, he mused; all her thoughts were with her companion and his peace of mind.

He could tell when Ahmed changed tack and started to talk about the expedition. Immediately Emma was reassuring him that it didn't matter. She glanced over at Seb for a few seconds and he guessed that Ahmed was saying she should continue as planned. He wondered if she would protest, but she just continued to nod.

Finally they embraced and after a few seconds Emma pushed the older man away, gesturing to his waiting brothers. Within a few minutes Ahmed had gone.

The enormity of the situation suddenly dawned on Seb. He was about to set out on an expedition with Emma into the desert with only Akil and Akins for company. If anyone found out they would be scandalised.

He crossed the courtyard in a few long strides and stopped by Emma's side.

'Ahmed told you he had to leave?' Emma asked.

Seb nodded.

'Poor Ahmed, he returns to Egypt after twenty-four years and instead of a happy reunion he's faced with his father's demise.'

'At least he will have the chance to say goodbye.'

Seb knew only too well how much it hurt to never get to say goodbye to a parent, to leave without ever seeing someone you loved again.

Emma nodded.

'You understand that without Ahmed it will just be the four of us?' Seb asked.

Emma turned towards him.

'You'll still take me?'

'If you wish. As long as you understand people might gossip.'

He saw a cloud pass over her face, but suddenly she brightened. 'Well, I can certainly handle a little bit of gossip. I was sure you were going to cancel the expedition.'

Seb shook his head. 'I probably should,' he murmured. 'Always was a bit of a fool.'

'And there's no reason for people to know Ahmed isn't with us. We can send word when we're almost back and it'll be as if he were there all along.'

Seb grimaced. 'People always find out, no matter what precautions are taken.'

'Still, if you're willing to take me, I would like to go. Even if people will gossip.'

Seb nodded curtly and turned to shout a couple of orders to Akil and Akins. They scuttled to the horse that was meant to be Ahmed's and quickly started to transfer bags.

'When do I get to see the map we're following?' Seb asked whilst they watched Akil and Akins work.

'What makes you think there's a map?'

Seb raised an eyebrow but didn't say any more. If she wasn't ready to trust him yet that was fine. She'd have to reveal their final destination eventually.

Within minutes the two young brothers had transferred the bags from Ahmed's horse and distributed them amongst the others. Seb spent a little while checking everything was to his satisfaction, then motioned for Emma to come closer.

'Ready?' he asked her.

'Ready.'

Expertly he boosted her up onto the horse and helped her adjust her dress so she was sitting comfortably.

'I've got a pair of breeches if you'd be more comfortable.'

Emma looked shocked and he laughed.

'Let's see what you think at the end of the first day of riding.'

When he was happy that she was safely perched in the saddle and capable of taking charge of her horse, Seb motioned for the boys to mount and then followed suit. He nudged his horse forward so he was side by side with Emma.

'Ready to start your Egyptian adventure?' he asked.

The smile on her face made Seb want to reach over and pull her into his lap, but, remembering his promise to Ahmed, instead he urged his horse forward and they set off.

Chapter Nine

Emma struggled to keep her eyes open. The sway of the horse beneath her and the warmth from the afternoon sun were enough to send anyone off to sleep. They'd been riding for hours, keeping a good steady pace. It had taken them almost the entire morning to get clear of Cairo and the villages that surrounded the city, and they had stopped for lunch just where the desert started in earnest. Then, Emma had been eager to push on, to get out into the desert proper. Now she was regretting taking the sights and sounds of Cairo for granted.

It wasn't that the desert was not stunning. In its own way, it was as beautiful as the rolling green hills of England. It was stark and striking and had its own charm. The problem was it all looked the same.

The only vegetation was a series of scraggy

bushes, which Emma wasn't convinced were still alive. The ground was mostly flat and it was an exciting moment when they climbed a few feet up a bank or descended into some long-dried-up river bed.

Most of the day Sebastian had kept her entertained. He'd talked of Egypt and some of his exploits—probably exaggerated, knowing Sebastian. And he'd talked of other explorers who had dedicated their lives to finding long-lost tombs and temples and even cities. But now he'd ridden off ahead to scout their route and find somewhere to stop for the night, and Emma was bored.

She mentally chastised herself. How could she even think she might be bored? She was here in Egypt, the country that had occupied her dreams for so long, and she was on an expedition to find the lost tomb of Telarti. This was the most exciting thing that had ever happened to her.

Squinting slightly into the sunlight, Emma wondered whether she could see Sebastian in the distance. She kept her eyes fixed on the tiny figure and smiled to herself as it started to take form. After a few minutes she could make out the strong contours of his torso and thighs, and after a few more his features started to come into focus. She found herself urging her horse to go just a little faster, eager to be back at Sebastian's side and hear what he had to say.

Ten minutes later Sebastian had reached them and fallen in at Emma's side. She looked at him inquisitively. He raised an eyebrow in question.

'So?' Emma asked eventually.

'So what?'

She sighed. 'What did you find?'

'A lot of sand. Few scrubby bushes. A dried-up river bed.'

Emma's face fell. 'We've got all that right here.'

Sebastian grinned. 'There may be something a little more interesting a few miles up ahead. You'll just have to wait and see.'

'You're not going to tell me?'

He shook his head. 'It would spoil the surprise.'

Emma huffed and squinted again into the distance, wondering whether she could make out a change in terrain at all.

'Don't strain your eyes. You won't be able to see anything for a while yet.'

'Is it where we will stop for the night?'

Sebastian nodded.

'Man-made or natural?'

He gave her a mock haughty stare. 'Madame will have to wait and see for herself.'

Emma returned to squinting at the horizon. From the corner of her eye she could see Sebastian grin, lean back as he relaxed and start to whistle. Sometimes the man could be infuriating. Emma resumed her purveyance of the horizon.

'Where was your father based when he was out here?' Sebastian asked suddenly.

Emma smiled in fond recollection of the stories her father had told her about his time in Egypt.

'He was based in Cairo, that was where they had a house, but he travelled around a lot. I think they were in Cairo only a few months of the year.'

'They?' Sebastian asked.

'My mother. They met here in Egypt. Father was overseeing some archaeological dig, Mother was out here with her family. She was the daughter of an English colonel in the army.'

Emma could almost picture the meeting, her father had told her about it so many times.

'Mama literally fell into the hole Father was

supervising the men to dig. He caught her and it was love at first sight.'

Emma couldn't imagine anything more romantic.

'They were married within six months. Father took Mama everywhere with him. They visited all the sights in Egypt and Mama even helped out on the digs he went to.'

'Sounds like a good life,' Sebastian said thoughtfully.

'It was. At least my father remembered it fondly. But then Mama fell pregnant with me.'

'And that's when they returned to England?'

Emma shook her head.

'They stayed here, despite what both their families wanted. Egypt was the home of their hearts, and they thought they wanted to raise me here.'

Sebastian remained silent, apparently aware this was a difficult and emotional subject for Emma to talk about.

'The birth was difficult, traumatic. Mama lost a lot of blood. She didn't ever get to hold me in her arms.'

Emma felt the tears spring to her eyes and tried to blink them away. Every time she thought of her poor mother she wondered what life would have been like if she'd survived.

'Father blamed himself, thought if he'd taken Mama back to England to give birth she would have lived. He boarded the first ship back home and didn't leave England again in his life.'

'It must have been difficult for him, raising you alone.'

Emma shrugged. 'I think for the first few years he struggled. He loved Mama so much he never got over the loss. But as I grew older he was the best father a girl could have.'

Sebastian reached over and took her hand in his own.

'He sounds like he was a great man and a wonderful father.'

Emma felt the warmth and reassurance of his touch and in that instant hoped he would never let go.

'When I was young, I used to catch him staring at maps of Egypt or examining scrolls or old books. I think he missed the country but could never bring himself to come back.'

'The memories of your mother would have been too overwhelming.'

Emma glanced at Sebastian. He was looking

out into the distance. She wondered whether he'd had a happy childhood growing up.

'When I was still a child I used to ask him to bring me here. I didn't realise how painful his memories were.'

'I'm sure he didn't mind you asking.'

Emma smiled at the memory. 'He used to make a joke of it, say I'd be eaten by a cursed mummy or kidnapped by bandits as soon as I stepped onto Egyptian soil.'

'Did he know you were planning on coming to Egypt?'

Emma shook her head. He hadn't known, at least not explicitly. But she wondered if deep down he'd always expected her to travel to the country he'd loved so much in his youth one day.

'I didn't really make any plans until after he died, after I'd come out of mourning.'

She remembered the instant she'd decided she was going to travel. It had been exciting and terrifying all at the same time. It wasn't what young ladies of society did, but Emma had felt less like a lady of society and more like an out-cast for a while. All she would be doing was giving the gossips something else to talk about.

'It's a very brave thing you did,' Sebastian said quietly. 'I don't know many women who would travel halfway across the world on their own.'

'Sometimes I feel like it's all a dream,' Emma confessed, 'and that soon I'll wake up in my bed in Kensington with nothing but memories.'

'We'd better make them good ones, then,' Sebastian said as he urged his horse forward.

She laughed and tried to keep up. They cantered along for a few minutes and Emma enjoyed the sensation of a warm breeze on her face. The desert seemed much more inviting when she had Sebastian to share it with.

They mounted a small ridge and Sebastian drew his horse in to a walk. Twenty seconds later Emma was by his side. She followed the direction of his gaze down into a shallow canyon and her breath caught in her throat.

'It's beautiful,' she said eventually.

About a mile away, along the bed of the canyon, the browns and yellows of the desert were interrupted by a splash of green. A dozen palm trees towered above the rolling dunes and on the desert floor the vegetation was thick and lush. Emma could just about make out a sliver of blue amongst the green.

'It's an oasis,' she said in amazement. 'I've never seen one before.'

'Want to get a closer look?'

In response Emma nudged her horse forward and started down the zigzagging path.

'This whole area used to be criss-crossed by rivers,' Sebastian explained. 'We're riding in a river bed now. Not that it's had any water in it for hundreds of years.'

'And the oasis is all that's left?'

Sebastian nodded sadly. 'One lone watering hole. Probably in another few hundred years even that won't exist.'

As they rode towards the oasis Emma could see the first proper signs of life since leaving Cairo. On the ground were a few dusty footprints, signs that other animals used the oasis as a watering hole.

In less than half an hour Sebastian motioned for Emma to stop and dismount. Carefully he led her through the bushes that surrounded the small pool of water. Taking Wadjet's reins, Sebastian quickly tied up the two horses where they could drink at their leisure. Both beasts started lapping greedily at the water and Sebastian laughed.

'Is it bad I feel like I want to do the same?' he asked, turning back to face Emma.

'I won't judge.'

She watched as he lowered himself to his knees and scooped some of the clear, fresh water into his hands. He drank for a long few seconds before motioning for her to join him.

Kneeling down next to him, Emma knew she was too close. Something about Sebastian made her lose all sense of reason, and crouching next to him in such close proximity only made things worse.

Wordlessly he refilled his hands with water and lifted them towards her lips. Long seconds passed as Emma tried to resist touching his hands with her mouth and taking a drink. It was to no avail. She wasn't that strong. She badly wanted the water, and what was worse was that she wanted to drink it from Sebastian's hands.

Her lips touched his skin and parted slightly, allowing the cool liquid to trickle into her mouth and down her throat. It was heavenly after so many hours of the dust and dirt of the desert. She felt cleansed and rejuvenated.

Once she had drained his hands Sebastian lowered them from her lips and dipped his palms again into the water. Emma's heart pounded in her chest as again he raised his flesh to her lips and motioned for her to drink. This time as the water slipped down her throat her eyes met Sebastian's and a flicker passed between them. She wanted him to cup her face with those strong hands and kiss her just as he had a week previously.

Emma held her breath as Sebastian seemed to sway towards her, his eyes locked on hers. His lips parted ever so slightly and his hands fell away from her mouth.

Then, as suddenly as it had begun, the moment passed. Sebastian pulled away, getting to his feet too quickly and almost overbalancing. Emma felt too stunned to move. Despite all of her self-recriminations she'd wanted Sebastian to kiss her again. She'd wanted to feel his mouth on hers and get lost in the heady sensation of desire and lust.

Her cheeks began to redden and Emma took the hand Sebastian was offering to her without looking at him. How could she be so foolish? Once was bad enough, but kissing the man twice would be unforgivable. Wanton. Everything the gossips had said about her would be proved to be true.

As soon as she was on her feet, Sebastian let go of her hand and turned away, fussing over the horses. Emma pushed away the faint pang of regret and steeled herself. She was a strong young woman who didn't need a man like Sebastian to kiss her to give purpose to her life.

With one last wistful look at Sebastian's back, Emma took a few steps away and began to explore the oasis. After all, this was her adventure. She wasn't going to let some inappropriate feelings for Sebastian spoil it.

Chapter Ten

Seb fiddled with the horses' reins, pretending to check they were secure. In reality he was trying to stop his head from spinning. He glanced over his shoulder. Emma had walked a couple of paces away and was examining the vegetation intently. He was sure she'd felt it too, the flare of attraction that had passed between them. One second he'd been offering her water to help her rehydrate, the next the movement of her lips to his hands had become the most sensual thing in the world.

He'd imagined cupping her face with his hands and bringing her full lips towards his until they met in an exquisite kiss. Every nerve in his body was on edge and firing, asking for more stimulation. He needed to stay in control, and when Emma was around that just didn't seem to happen.

Seb shook his head. He'd known a two-week expedition into the desert with Emma was a bad idea when he'd accepted the job offer. She was alluring and arousing and he didn't seem to be able to keep his hands off her.

The plea from Ahmed earlier in the day rang in his ears, but in truth Seb didn't need the older man's words to know any liaison with Emma was wrong. She was a well-brought-up young woman who had been unfortunate enough to be tainted by one scandal in her life—the last thing she needed was a second. But more than that, Seb should be shunning any thought of romantic involvement with her. He had seen what men of his family turned into when they married, he had seen the destructive relationship between his father and mother, and he wasn't about to follow in their footsteps. Seb would never know what kind of a husband he would make, but to him never knowing was better than being a husband like his father had been. The family resemblance was strong. He was like his father in so many ways; what was to say he wouldn't be like his father towards women, too?

No, the safest thing for Seb was to continue to limit his romantic involvement with women to short dalliances, affairs with an end date firmly stamped upon them; that way he wouldn't hurt anyone. Not the way his father had hurt his mother.

Seb shuddered as he remembered the first time he'd seen his father raise a fist to his sweet, loving mother. She'd cowered away, but had not fled, as if she knew what was expected of her. In his darkest moments Sebastian wondered whether he could ever be so cruel, and knew he could never risk finding out. There had been occasions when a rage had descended over him and he had found it hard to control. He'd never hurt a woman, or even hit someone in anything but self-defence, but he couldn't ever risk letting anyone get close, in case he did hurt them.

He would just have to curb his attraction towards Emma and act the role of a professional guide. Once this expedition was over, the best thing would be to never see her again.

Akins and Akil shattered the peace of the oasis with their animated chatter and for a few moments Sebastian was thankful of the distraction they provided.

'Four men on horseback, trailing at a distance of two miles,' Akins said as he came to a stop before Seb.

'They are slow and stupid,' Akil added.

Seb nodded slowly. He'd been aware they were being followed whilst they were still in the streets of Cairo. When they'd entered the desert he'd sent Akil and Akins to flank the men following them and gain more information.

'Either they're slow and stupid or they don't mind us knowing they are following us,' Seb said quietly.

He glanced at the sun. It was starting to dip towards the horizon; they probably had an hour, maybe two at most until sunset. Night-time in the desert descended quickly.

'We need to keep watch throughout the night,' Seb said. 'Hopefully they will keep their distance and just continue to observe for now.'

'Akil, you will take the first watch...' Seb paused as he calculated '...four hours. Then I will take the second. Akins, you will relieve me and watch until dawn.'

The boys nodded.

'Go and set up an observation point near the top of the canyon, before the path leads down into the dried-up river bed. They will have to pass by to reach our camp.'

Akil and Akins scurried off back the way they came. Although they were young, barely more than children, Seb knew he could rely on the two brothers as much as he could anyone in his employ. Four years ago he'd intervened when they'd been caught stealing. Some fast talking on his part had helped them avoid a harsh penalty, and they'd been his loyal employees ever since. He'd never known either of them to fall asleep whilst on watch or to disobey an order.

Seb turned to face Emma, knowing he was going to have to talk to her at some point— delaying the conversation would only make it more awkward. She was looking wistfully at the clear pool of water as if she wanted nothing more than to dive in.

'The boys have gone to set up an observation post,' Seb said. 'If you want to bathe you'll have complete privacy.'

Emma looked from him back to the water dubiously.

'Could there be crocodiles?' she asked.

Sebastian laughed. 'All this way in the desert with nothing to eat? Unlikely.'

She still didn't look sure.

'I can go first to put your mind at ease.'

She didn't move, but continued to look at the water. Suddenly Seb wanted nothing more than to strip off and dive into the crisp, clear water. The day's ride through the desert hadn't been exhausting, but it had been hot and sticky and he wanted to feel refreshed and cool.

Without another word he started to slowly strip off. Emma seemed frozen, her eyes roaming over his body as he raised his hands to start unfastening his garments. As he pulled his shirt over his head, revealing his tanned torso below, he thought he heard a little intake of breath from Emma. He hooked his thumbs into the waistband of his trousers and gave her a long hard look.

'I will be naked when I take these down,' Sebastian said.

For a second Emma didn't move, just stared at the point where his thumbs disappeared into his trousers, then she seemed to realise exactly where she was looking and spun around so quickly Seb thought she might fall over.

He chuckled quietly to himself; at least he hadn't lost the ability to shock a well-brought-up young lady. Quickly he divested himself of the rest of his clothes and left them in a pile by the water's edge. With a glance around to check Emma wasn't peeking, he started to stride into the water.

It was cool against his skin and Seb knew he'd have a hard time persuading his tired muscles to get out of the small pool. When he was submerged to the waist he took a deep breath and dived under the water, enjoying the sensation of complete submergence and the eerie silence underwater.

He surfaced and turned back towards Emma, just quick enough to see the swish of her skirt as she turned back around. She'd been peeking.

Seb grinned, found his footing and stood, letting the water drip from his torso. He was decent, nothing south of his waist was visible, so he thought he might have a bit of fun with the peeking Miss Knight.

Seb let out a strained roar and started splashing in the water. When he was sure he'd got Emma's attention he ducked his head under, just leaving his arms splashing on the surface. After a few seconds he became completely still. He stayed that way for ten more seconds then surfaced.

Emma was in the process of unfastening her dress, her fingers slipping on all the ties. When Seb resurfaced she froze and shot him a disbelieving look.

'I thought you were drowning,' she said, a hint of anger in her voice.

'You were coming to save me?'

Emma looked to where her fingers were still pulling at the laces of her dress and shrugged. 'I need my guide to be alive.'

'Well, I've explored every inch of this pool and I can assure you there are no crocodiles in here.'

Emma nodded and Seb realised she was staring again at his bare chest. It was as though she'd never seen a man half naked before. Seb grinned; maybe she hadn't. Maybe her single night with Freddie hadn't extended to examining the male form. The idea made him feel more pleased than it should. He stretched, then bobbed farther down in the water.

'It's lovely and cool. Why don't you come in?'

Emma looked at him as though he were mad.

'Come in?' she asked. 'With you?'

He nodded. He was already regretting the invitation. It had just slipped out, a manifestation of his subconscious and the part of him that wanted her naked in the water with him.

'That would be scandalous.'

Seb shrugged. 'There's no one here to tell.'

Emma looked around her just to confirm they were alone.

'I won't look as you get in,' Seb said. 'On my honour.'

Emma had slipped off her heavy boots and cautiously dipped a toe into the water. Seb could tell it must have felt heavenly against her skin as she sighed and closed her eyes.

'I could wait until you get out,' Emma said, a sliver of doubt creeping into her voice.

'It'll be getting dark soon,' Seb said. 'If you're happy swimming in the dark…'

She glanced at the sky and noted the position of the dropping sun.

'I suppose if you stick to your half…'

Seb grinned. She was coming in. He knew he should be a gentleman and insist he get out, then turn his back whilst she bathed, but he wasn't that strong a man. He wanted there to be nothing more than the cool water between their bodies.

'Turn around,' Emma said. 'And no peeking.'

Seb saluted and turned so his back was facing Emma. The noises she made as she undressed were tantalising in the extreme and Seb was sorely tempted to break his promise and take a quick look, but he kept his feet squarely planted on the ground and his eyes facing forward. He heard the rustle of her skirts and imagined her lifting the dusty dress over her head, and then a quieter sound, which Seb could only conclude were her undergarments being removed.

'Can I turn around yet?' Seb asked, his voice almost catching in his throat.

He wanted her to say yes, he wanted to see her silhouetted against the darkening sky, naked and in all her glory.

'No,' Emma said firmly.

Seb sighed.

He heard a splashing sound, then a sharp intake of breath followed by some more splashing.

'Sebastian,' Emma said eventually. 'You can turn around now.'

Seb spun slowly, wondering what he was going to see. Emma was submerged up to her shoulders; just the milky skin of her neck was visible above the water.

'This is heavenly,' she said.

Seb had to agree. He couldn't tear his eyes away. He wanted nothing more than for Emma to place her feet on the ground and slowly stand up.

'I could stay in here all night,' Emma murmured.

'When the sun goes down it'll get cold quickly. The last place you'll want to be is in the water then.'

'After the heat of today I can't ever imagine being cold again.'

Seb laughed and leaned back in the water. He watched as Emma started to unfasten the pins that held her hair in place and let the soft blonde locks fall about her shoulders. She looked like a siren arising from the depths, ready to lure unsuspecting men in and captivate them with her charms.

Once she'd shaken the last of her hair free from its constraints, Seb watched as she leaned back in the water and dipped her head under, submerging her hair and most of her face. When she surfaced her hair was slicked back by the water and Emma drew in a long, deep breath to replenish her lungs. Seb wondered if he'd ever seen anything so erotic.

He was in a dangerous situation. As he had desired, the only thing separating him from Emma was a few feet of water. It would take no effort at all to swim a couple of strokes and press her naked body up against his. He felt the first stirrings of arousal and knew he had to get out of the water and put some clothes back on before he did something they both regretted.

'I should make a fire before it gets dark,' Seb said gruffly.

Emma just stared at him, her eyes wide and droplets of water snaking down her forehead.

'I'm going to get out now,' he said.

She didn't move.

He stood, revealing his entire torso. Emma was staring at him as though she couldn't look away.

'In twenty seconds I will be out of the water,' he warned.

Emma's eyes met his, but still she didn't turn away.

'And I'm not wearing a thing,' he reminded her gently.

A small gush of air escaped Emma's lips, her eyes widened and hurriedly she turned around, allowing him some privacy to exit the water. Seb felt a stab of disappointment, but knew it was for the best. He knew he should get out and get dressed and start the fire, and forget about Emma's naked form a few feet away.

Chapter Eleven

Emma languished in the cool water, feeling all the dust and dirt from the long day's ride being washed away, and she felt rejuvenated. She could hear Sebastian thrashing around somewhere behind her and opened one eye. Maybe it wouldn't be so bad if she took just one little look.

Emma had never seen a man naked before. In fact she'd never even seen a man half naked before Sebastian had stood there with his torso exposed. The sight had sent sparks of heat down to her abdomen and now she was craving more.

When she had been duped by Freddie into giving herself to him it had been a hurried affair. Neither of them had undressed. Freddie had just pushed her to the bed and lifted her skirts. She hadn't seen a single bit of flesh that she wouldn't see at a ball or dinner party.

Not that Freddie's physique could ever be compared to Sebastian's, clothed or unclothed. Sebastian was muscled and powerful and every inch of skin Emma had caught a glimpse of was tanned to a beautiful bronze colour.

Emma placed her feet on the bottom of the pool and slowly started to turn around, making sure she kept her shoulders under the water.

Sebastian had pulled on his trousers and was standing with his back to her. She could see tiny rivulets of water trickling down between his shoulder blades. She wanted nothing more than to reach out and touch them, to trail her fingers over the taut muscles of his back and find out if they really were as firm as they looked.

Suddenly Sebastian froze and slowly turned back towards her. Emma knew she wouldn't be able to turn around in time. His eyes locked onto hers and she could see the desire flaring just beneath the surface.

Emma felt as though she were on fire. She wanted to be brazen and bold, but a tiny voice of reason was holding her back. She wanted to stand and walk over to Sebastian, allow his eyes to roam over her naked body, then she wanted to press herself against him.

As soon as she thought it Emma knew it

could never be. It was the same mistake she'd made with Freddie all over again. And Sebastian might be a better man than Freddie, but it still wouldn't make any sort of intimacy right.

Emma tried to look away but her eyes didn't seem to want to obey any command. She was frozen in place, her eyes locked with Sebastian's, her desire for him building every second she stayed still.

Eventually Sebastian's lips formed the now familiar grin and the connection was broken.

'You peeked, Miss Knight,' Sebastian said, his voice low and dangerous.

Emma nodded, not knowing what else to say.

'Surely if you peeked, then I'm allowed to?'

Emma felt an unexpected thrill at the idea of standing naked in front of Sebastian and letting him peruse her body with his eyes. She opened her mouth to respond but no sound came out.

Sebastian watched her and Emma wondered if he was really expecting her to stand naked in front of him.

'Sometimes I hate being a gentleman,' Sebastian said, his voice low and almost dangerous. Slowly he turned around. 'I'd hurry if I were you, Miss Knight. I don't know how long my resolve will hold.'

Emma forced the muscles in her legs to move and stood, shivering slightly as the evening air cooled her skin and caused it to tighten and pucker. Quickly she made her way out of the water and struggled to pull her dress over her wet body.

'Dry yourself first,' Sebastian said gruffly, throwing a coarse blanket in her direction. 'Otherwise you'll catch a chill.'

Emma picked it up and started to rub herself dry, keeping one eye on Sebastian at all times to check his back was firmly towards her. Once she was no more than damp she tried again to get her dress on over her head. She struggled for a few minutes to straighten all the material against her damp skin, turning round in circles to try and untangle the skirts.

She stopped dead as she felt Sebastian's hands on her shoulders and didn't even dare to breathe as he helped her fasten the dress. His breath was warm against her neck and sent shivers down her spine. Sebastian worked in silence, his fingers deftly doing what Emma's hadn't been able to. When he stepped away, Emma felt almost bereft and turned to face him.

Sebastian was standing a few feet away looking at her strangely. As she watched he roused himself, shook his head and started to move.

'We need to gather firewood,' he said.

Emma nodded, glad of something practical to do. She slipped her feet back into her boots and ventured off into the undergrowth. After five minutes she returned with a pile of sticks. Sebastian nodded approvingly and took them from her. Whilst she had been away, he had been busy starting a small fire. The flames were crackling as they consumed the leaves and small twigs he fed onto it.

'Good. With these, the fire should last most of the night.'

Emma watched as he fed a larger stick onto the fire then sat back, seemingly satisfied with his work.

'Hungry?' he asked.

Emma nodded, realising she was starving. They hadn't had anything to eat since midday and, although it wasn't the most strenuous of exercise, riding through the desert had given her quite an appetite.

Sebastian gave her two pots to fill with water and instructed her how to build a stand to balance them above the fire. When the water was bubbling away nicely, they added a small portion of rice, seasoned with herbs, to one pot. To the second pot Sebastian added some salted fish.

'It won't be the kind of meal you're used to.'

Emma breathed in the scent of the cooking food. 'I don't think I've ever smelt anything more tempting,' she said.

It was the truth. There was something magical about cooking their dinner above an open fire in an oasis in Egypt. Emma wouldn't have cared if it were just plain rice they were cooking. It still would have been a wonderful meal.

As if summoned by the scent, Akil came scurrying through the trees towards the campfire. When the rice and fish were cooked, Sebastian dished up two portions and handed them to Akil. He disappeared the way he'd come, taking his brother his evening meal.

Sebastian served the remaining two portions and handed one to Emma. She took the metal tin and inhaled deeply. The rice was seasoned to perfection and the fish still had a salty tang in its aroma.

Sitting on the ground with her skirts gathered up around her, Emma started to eat. Each mouthful was pure bliss, and she wasn't sure whether it was the surroundings or the fact she was so hungry that transformed the simple meal into something so delicious.

They ate in silence, and after they had finished Emma collected the used plates and pots and rinsed them with water from the pool.

'Stay close to the fire overnight,' Sebastian said.

Emma looked at the tree line behind her and wondered for the first time what kind of wild animals there were in Egypt.

Sebastian grinned at her expression and started to build the fire up so it would keep them warm overnight.

'Probably the most dangerous animal in the desert is the scorpion,' Sebastian said. 'But you also have to watch out for snakes.'

Emma nodded and huddled in closer to the fire. Now it was dark, the air seemed to have a chill to it and she quickly went about fastening her damp hair up and away from her shoulders. Sebastian tossed her the small sack she was keeping her change of clothes in and instructed her to use it as a pillow. Silently Emma laid down and watched the flames.

Sebastian stood and walked over to her and gently covered her over with a coarse woollen blanket. Immediately Emma felt the benefit and burrowed down underneath it.

'Where will you be sleeping?' Emma asked.

'Just here.' He indicated a spot only a couple of feet away. If she desired she would be able to reach out in the night and touch him. Emma wasn't sure if it was a good thing or not. 'The boys will sleep on the other side of the fire.'

The ground was hard, but Emma soon forgot the discomfort as she stared up at the night's sky. There was not a single cloud in sight, just hundreds of stars shining so brightly they hurt her eyes if she looked too long.

'It's beautiful,' she said sleepily. 'I'm not sure I could ever sleep with a sky like that to look at.'

Sebastian laughed as her eyes began to droop and Emma surrendered her body to sleep. Her last thought before oblivion was how nice it would be to have Sebastian's firm body cradling hers and keeping her safe.

Chapter Twelve

Sebastian awoke with a soft groan. He wasn't as young as he used to be, and a night sleeping on the hard ground took him longer to recover from. He shifted slightly, then froze. Something warm and soft was pressing up against his side. Cautiously he opened one eye and glanced down—sure enough, the soundly sleeping form of Miss Knight was flush against him.

He wondered how it had happened. He remembered returning in the small hours of the morning and wearily taking his place back by the glowing embers of the fire. He must have misjudged it and fallen asleep much closer to Emma than he had planned. And now she was burrowing in closer, doing nothing to curb the desire that was already burning so strongly inside him.

She was still fast asleep, and he took a moment to enjoy the sensation. It was a long time since he had woken up to the soft form of a woman beside him. In his desire to keep his liaisons as short-lived as possible he rarely spent the night with a woman.

Emma was beautiful in the first morning rays of sunlight. Her cheeks had a slight rosy tint and her eyelashes rested gracefully on her cheeks. Her hair was falling out of the up-do she had secured it into the night before and curled a little as it fell around her shoulders. Sebastian's eyes trailed lower. The modest neckline of Emma's dress had slipped a little in her sleep, and although nothing was exposed he caught a glimpse of the creamy white skin of her chest.

He groaned. He knew he should move. If Emma awoke to find herself in this position she would be mortified. Although…Sebastian shook his head. No matter how interested she had seemed in his naked form the night before, that didn't give him an excuse to prolong their closeness—if anything it was all the more reason to move away.

Stealthily Sebastian eased himself away from Emma's still-slumbering form and stood, stretching and yawning as he stepped away.

He watched as Emma's eyes fluttered open

and couldn't help but smile at the slight frown on her face as she tried to work out where she was. Then all the memories from the day before must have come flooding back as she sat hurriedly and rubbed the last remnants of sleep from her eyes. She straightened her dress, concealing that hint of cleavage, and stretched her arms above her head.

'I can't believe I slept so well,' she said. 'I never expected to get more than a few hours.'

'Sleeping in the open air is good for you,' Sebastian said cheerily. 'And you would have been tired after the day's ride.'

Emma nodded. Sebastian went over to the pack with the food supplies in and took out one of the pots he used to heat water over the fire. He grabbed a stick and pushed the embers around. They weren't hot, just warm.

'Your coffee will be lukewarm, I'm afraid. We haven't got time to build up the fire again.'

He filled the pot with water and placed it on the embers, allowing the residual heat from the fire to seep through and warm the water. Then he added a generous spoonful of coffee.

Sebastian returned to his pack and brought out two small loaves of flat, dried bread. Gently he shook Akil awake and handed him one of the loaves. Then he split the remaining bread in half and walked towards Emma.

Silently they sat by the pool of the oasis and ate their breakfast.

'I don't think I'll ever forget this,' Emma said when she had finished eating.

Sebastian had to admit it was beautiful; the reflection of the early morning sun was shimmering on the surface of the water and the trees of the oasis cast long shadows around them.

After breakfast Sebastian quickly set about packing up the horses. He was eager for an early start. No doubt the men who had been following them would wake up with the dawn and set off soon after. At least there had been no sign of their approach through the night. For now at least, their pursuers seemed content just to trail them.

Sebastian wondered again just what it was Emma had in her possession, and how these men had got to know about it. He doubted they were interested purely for the historical interest of whatever it was they were seeking out and knew that more likely than not they would be dangerous. He suspected there would be a confrontation before the trip was finished. At the moment he wasn't sure how they would come out on top, but he was working on a solution.

Just as Akil and Akins rode their horses back into their small camp Sebastian surveyed the scene and nodded in satisfaction. The fire was nothing more than a pile of ash now, no threat to the little oasis they would be leaving behind.

He ushered Emma over to her horse and made a cup with his hand to boost her onto the seat. She had just placed her foot into his hands when she let out a strangled scream.

Sebastian froze; the sound cut through his heart like ice. Quickly he looked her over. There was no sign of blood or a bullet wound, but he couldn't be sure.

'My leg,' Emma whimpered.

Sebastian gently lowered her to the ground under the watchful eyes of Akil and Akins. Emma grabbed at her left calf and Sebastian felt the panic leave him. She hadn't been shot or mortally injured; she had cramp. Her muscles had protested at the idea of another day spent in the saddle and they had seized up.

Cautiously he lifted her skirt so he exposed her leg to the knee. Emma looked at him with wide eyes but allowed him to continue. Firmly he pressed his hands against the flesh of her calf, massaging and stretching to try and relieve the taut muscle. Emma bit her lip at first as the pain continued, but with Sebastian's constant ministrations after a few seconds the muscle relaxed and Emma gave a big sigh of relief.

'Thank you,' she said. 'I thought my leg was about to explode.'

Sebastian laughed.

'It was cramp,' he explained. 'A muscle spasm. It's because you're not used to riding for so long. The muscle is tired and is letting you know.'

Emma nodded and looked down at where his hands were still kneading the muscle of her calf.

Sebastian quickly stood and backed away, allowing Emma to pull her skirt back to her ankles.

'Shall we try that again?' he asked, motioning to the horse.

This time he deposited Emma in the saddle without any problems, untied her horse then quickly mounted his own. Within a few minutes they had left the oasis behind them and were striking out farther south into the desert.

'I give in,' Emma said as she lowered herself to the ground. 'I don't know how women are expected to ride all day in such heavy skirts.'

Seb eyed her appraisingly. Her attire was unsuitable for the desert. He knew the best thing you could wear was a long, loose robe, as the locals did. Emma's dress was long but it certainly wasn't loose. The bodice constricted her torso and the layers of skirts got wrapped around her legs every time she tried to manoeuvre. The second best thing you could wear in the desert was a comfortable pair of trousers and a loose shirt that covered as much skin as possible from the burning rays of the sun.

'The offer still stands,' Seb said. 'I have some trousers and a shirt you're most welcome to wear.'

Emma looked at him thoughtfully, as if carefully weighing up the pros and cons. Seb could just imagine her perched up on the horse with a pair of trousers stretched tight around her womanly curves, the material outlining perfectly the contours of her buttocks and thighs. He swallowed. Maybe he should be discouraging her from taking him up on his offer. He found her far too attractive for his own good already, when most of her figure was hidden under the skirts of her dress.

'Maybe I could try them just for this afternoon, see if a change of clothing really would make a difference to my comfort?'

Seb dismounted, handed the reins of his horse to Akil and started rummaging through one of his packs.

'The trousers might be a bit on the long side,' he said, eyeing up Emma's petite form, 'and the shirt a little baggy.' He handed her the two garments and a belt.

Emma looked around them. They had stopped for lunch in the shade of a bush. Seb looked at the scraggy mass of branches—maybe a bush was a bit generous. Whatever it was it didn't give them much protection from the sun, and it certainly didn't provide privacy for changing. There wasn't another bush for as far as the eye could see, or anything else that would shield Emma from prying eyes.

Seb spoke quickly to Akil and Akins in Arabic. He instructed them to walk the horses slowly for two hundred paces in the opposite direction.

'You've got about four minutes until the boys turn around.'

Emma still didn't move.

'What about you?' she asked.

'I thought I'd help,' Seb said with a grin.

He almost laughed at her horrified expression and slowly turned his body so he was facing away from her. After twenty seconds of silence he heard the rustling of material as she began to divest herself of her dress. Seb was sorely tempted to turn around. At the oasis he had behaved like the perfect gentleman, not peeking at her once whilst she emerged from the pool despite having caught her staring at him. Now his resolve was weakened, every minute he spent with her he seemed to want her more, the desire was bubbling away beneath the surface and soon he knew it would boil over. Perhaps one look, one peek, would be enough to keep him purely simmering for a while longer.

'Ooh…ow!' he heard from behind him.

It was the excuse he had been waiting for. He spun around. Emma was standing a couple of feet away, her dress lifted up so it obscured her face. She wasn't naked in front of him, a thin chemise covered most of her, but the cotton was flattened against her body and Seb could see every curve and contour. He took a step towards her, telling himself he should just turn back around but not able to comply. Emma had got one of the fastenings of her dress caught in her hair and was now struggling to free it. The dress wouldn't go up over her head or pull back down and Seb could see the more she struggled, the worse she was making the situation.

He crossed over to her in two short strides and stilled her with his arms. He heard her gasp at the contact but she didn't protest. Gently he untangled the fastening from her hair and lifted the dress off over her head.

Emma lifted her eyes to his and they stood locked together for a few seconds. She was looking at him with such desire burning in her eyes Seb knew he wouldn't be able to refuse her anything. Slowly he reached out with his hand and placed it on her waist, flattening the chemise against her skin. He could feel the heat radiating from her as he pulled her closer towards him and he revelled in the easy way in which her body moulded against his. Emma tilted her chin upwards and, with his arm still holding her firmly in place, Seb lowered his mouth onto hers. Her lips were moist and sweet and inviting. Seb kissed her gently at first, but as she let out a soft moan his kiss became more urgent and all-encompassing. As she parted her lips he gently dipped his tongue inside her mouth and elicited another groan of pleasure.

As he kissed her Seb's hands started to caress her body. He wanted to remember every curve and every touch. His fingers glided over her softly rounded buttocks and then back to her narrow waist and then up to her shoulders, retracing their steps on the return journey.

As Seb's hand rested again on Emma's buttocks it slowly dawned on him what he was doing. He was seducing her. He was ruining her. He was doing everything he'd promised himself he wouldn't.

Gently he pulled away and put a step between them. He knew the minute Emma saw the regret in his eyes. Her expression changed from one of happiness to embarrassment and anger. Quickly she covered herself with her arms and started to tug on the trousers beneath her chemise. Seb ached to help her, to caress her thighs as he pulled the trousers up over her legs and secured them around her perfect waist, but he knew that would only make things worse.

'Turn around,' Emma said, her voice nearly breaking on the first word.

Seb wanted to reach out and touch her, pull her towards him again and kiss her so deeply she'd forget she was angry with him, but he knew he couldn't. Kissing her once was a mistake, twice unforgivable. Kissing her a third time would just be cruel to both of them.

Chapter Thirteen

Emma felt lonely. The desert was deathly quiet. Only the pad of the horses' hooves disturbed the silence, and she'd been listening to that for so long it had faded into the background. She glanced over to where Sebastian was riding a few paces in front of her. He hadn't said a word since they'd stopped for lunch, since they'd kissed. More significantly he hadn't smiled once. The man who always had a grin on his face and a joke on his lips now looked deadly serious.

She didn't understand why he was so upset now. It was he who had initiated the kiss, not her. He'd come to her assistance without her even asking him to, and he'd bent his head and covered her mouth with his. He could have untangled her dress from her hair and then turned his back; it wasn't as if she'd forced him to kiss her. So she didn't understand why he was quite so distant now.

It should be her that was angry. He'd pounced on her! Emma grimaced—pounced wasn't the right word. If she was honest with herself, she had been dreaming of kissing Sebastian ever since she'd locked eyes with him on the banks of the Nile. But she hadn't done anything about it.

She glanced over at him again. He was as still as a statue and had the same stony expression fixed on his face.

The worst thing was she didn't regret their kiss, at least not as much as she should do. Kissing Sebastian was a bad idea, that much she knew. He wasn't the kind of man you settled down with, and getting married was a dream Emma had given up on long ago. Which meant kissing Sebastian was nothing more than a dalliance, a flirtation. She had been hurt before by letting a man take too many liberties with her affections; she'd thought she had learned her lesson.

Clearly not. If she was truthful with herself Emma knew she would kiss him again. Sebastian would only have to narrow his eyes, pull her towards him and she would submit to him.

It was a different situation from what had

happened with Freddie. Freddie had promised to marry her and she'd thought giving herself to him would keep him interested, prompt him to announce the engagement he had made her keep secret. Instead all the man had wanted was a tumble between the sheets. Once he had got what he wanted she had never seen him again.

No, Sebastian was very different from Freddie, but he still hadn't promised her anything. If she allowed any further intimacies there was no knowing where it would lead. He had no obligation to marry her, and Emma wouldn't ever want to be the woman who forced a man down the aisle.

The only solution was to not allow anything intimate to happen again. Twice was unforgivable, but three times would be disastrous. Emma watched as Sebastian stretched in the saddle and took a deep breath in. She would have to be strong. She couldn't deny the force of the attraction she felt for him, which meant each and every time they were together she would have to remind herself why kissing him was a bad idea.

Emma nodded to herself and tightened her hold on the reins. She was resolved. She would admit her attraction and move on. From now on their relationship would be purely professional.

And if her resolve weakened she would remind herself of the months of hurt and heartache she'd suffered when Freddie had disappeared, taking her reputation with him. She had cried for two days solidly and the hurt and pain had lingered on for much, much longer. She couldn't bear to be in the same situation again—neither her heart nor her reputation would withstand it.

They had been riding for hours now without any respite. Emma had finished the last drop of water from her water skin over an hour ago and her throat was dry and itchy. The sun was dipping low in the sky and she knew they would have to stop and make camp soon, otherwise they would be riding in the dark.

She was just about to spur her horse forward so she was level with Sebastian when he raised a hand and motioned for her to look in front of them. Emma squinted into the distance and thought she could make out a shape near the horizon.

'We'll make camp there,' Sebastian said. 'It'll be close but we should just make it before sunset.'

'What is it?' Emma asked, glad to have something normal and mundane to talk about.

'Ruins.'

'Ruins? All the way out here?'

'It used to be a temple, provided shelter and sanctuary for weary travellers.'

'Very apt,' Emma said. She didn't think she'd ever been more weary in her life.

'There's only one wall still standing, and a few fallen columns, but it's as good a place to camp as any.'

Emma nodded.

'It'll be cold tonight,' Sebastian warned. 'There's no wood to fuel a fire and the sky is clear.'

They rode on in silence, watching the ruined temple take form before their eyes. Emma felt a bubble of excitement as she did every time she came across a temple or a tomb. It didn't matter how poor a state it was in, she still loved discovering nooks and crannies and picturing the ruins in their former glory.

After another forty minutes of riding they arrived at the temple. Sebastian was right: it was little more than a single wall with a few weather-beaten stones lying in piles in a seemingly haphazard pattern. There were a few columns lying on their sides in the middle of the structure.

Sebastian dismounted and reached up to help Emma down. His touch was feather-light and as soon as her feet touched the floor he moved away.

Emma took a few minutes to stretch out her sore muscles. She had always enjoyed riding but had hardly spent more than an hour at a time on a horse before. These long days of riding were punishing on her leg and back muscles.

Changing into Sebastian's trousers and shirt had been a godsend, and her afternoon ride had been much more comfortable than the morning; however, now she had dismounted she felt a little exposed clad only in trousers and a shirt. She was aware of the material of the trousers clinging to her buttocks and hips as she moved, and outlining the flesh below. Wearily Emma shook her head; she shouldn't worry too much. Sebastian had made it clear kissing her again was a mistake; he hadn't said a word all afternoon, just ridden along beside her in brooding silence. Emma wasn't so naive as to think his response meant he didn't desire her—a man didn't kiss a woman with that much passion and intensity twice without some desire involved—but he most certainly had regretted the kiss. Which meant he would be staying well away from her trouser-clad body. And Akil and Akins were barely more than children, more preoccupied with their games and competitions that kept them occupied during the long rides than her attire.

Already Sebastian and the boys were setting up the camp for the night, shaking out blankets and putting in place the bundles on which they rested their head. Emma glanced at the sky and saw it would be dark soon; the sun was already low and dipping fast. She'd noticed the sunsets were much quicker in Egypt than they were in England. It seemed as if one minute the sun was just starting its descent, the next it had fallen below the horizon.

Seeing that Sebastian had all the camp arrangements in hand, Emma went to explore the ruins. She spent a few minutes clambering over the fallen columns and inspecting the blocks of stone. On one or two there was just a hint of colour, a faded clue as to the vibrant paintwork that would have once covered the temple. Emma traced her fingers over the rough stone and closed her eyes, imagining she were back two thousand years and the temple were bustling with priests and visitors, humming with life.

Emma's eyes sprang open as someone touched her gently on the shoulder. She spun to find herself face to face with Sebastian.

'Isn't it beautiful?' he said, motioning at the horizon.

Emma glanced up and almost gasped. In just a few short minutes the sky had turned from blue to an assortment of reds and pinks.

'Come here,' Sebastian said, taking her hand and leading her to one of the fallen columns. He effortlessly lifted her up so she was sitting comfortably on it and pulled himself up beside her.

'I love the sunsets in the desert.'

Emma was just glad he was speaking to her. Anything was better than the silence of the afternoon. Sebastian was normally such a chatty person, always ready with a joke or a story to keep her entertained. The afternoon had seemed quiet and empty without his company.

They watched in silence as the sun continued its descent and Emma marvelled at the changing colours of the sky. Sebastian wasn't touching her but she could feel his presence and she sensed his tenseness.

'I apologise for earlier,' he said as the last rays of light disappeared.

Emma nodded, not knowing how else to respond.

'I acted without thinking.' He paused. 'No, I

acted on my base desires,' he corrected himself. 'And that was unacceptable.'

Emma still didn't say anything.

'I saw you all tangled up in that dress and I had an overwhelming urge to kiss you. But a gentleman would have restrained himself. You deserve better.'

He was speaking stiffly, as if the words were rehearsed. Emma wondered if this was what he'd been doing all afternoon—figuring out what to say to her.

'The thing is, you are a woman of good birth and I know it is expected that if a man compromises a woman in any way then he should do the right thing and marry her...' Sebastian raked a hand through his hair '...but I can't. It's not you—you're a wonderful woman and any man would be lucky to have you as his wife. It's just I won't marry. I can't marry.'

Emma nodded automatically. So this was what he was worrying about: that she'd force his hand and march him down the aisle. She would never expect him to propose just because they'd shared two unwitnessed kisses. She could put his mind at ease and hopefully they could go back to the way it had been before.

A small voice screamed inside her head, asking whether she really wanted things to go back to the way they were. And why didn't he want to marry her? What was so repulsive that two men metaphorically ran for the hills after a bit of intimacy?

'I'm sorry,' Sebastian finished quietly.

Emma took a deep breath and turned to face Sebastian. He was a good man; she'd come to realise that in the short time they'd spent together, and he'd never set out to seduce or delude her. They'd made a mistake, and he was trying to be honest and open about the consequences.

'No one but the two of us know about the kiss,' Emma said, seeking out his eyes in the darkness, 'so there's no need to even think of marriage. In the eyes of the world you haven't compromised me, and in my eyes I'm just as much to blame as you.'

Emma felt him relax a little beside her. She felt a pang of sadness at the thought of him regretting their moment of intimacy so much he'd had to spend a whole afternoon wondering how to tell her he wouldn't marry her.

'Thank you,' he said, his voice low and a little husky.

He jumped down from the column and reached up to help Emma down.

'I'm just going to stay for a minute longer,' Emma said.

Sebastian walked away back to where they'd laid out the camp and Emma was left alone. She felt the tears starting to form in her eyes and slip down her cheeks and she slowly brushed them away. She'd always thought what had happened with Freddie was an unfortunate lapse of judgement on her part, an episode that could have happened to any naive young girl. But now this had happened with Sebastian it made her think maybe it was something about her that was wrong. Firstly, after what had happened with Freddie she should know better than to kiss a man she barely knew, but Sebastian only had to look at her with his cheeky smile and piercing eyes and she knew she'd be back in his arms. Secondly, what was it about her that scared men off so completely? She'd never had a chance to confront Freddie, never known the whole truth about why he had done what he'd done, but she wondered now if it was because of something wrong with her.

Emma dried the tears from her cheeks and sniffed. She was stronger than this. She had long ago given up on the idea of a knight in shining armour coming to rescue her from the scandal and whisk her away to a life of married bliss. Instead she'd created new dreams, and one of them had been to explore Egypt. Now here she was, and she was determined not to let any man get in the way of that.

Chapter Fourteen

Seb rolled over and opened his eyes. He'd given up trying to sleep hours ago. He had taken the first watch, setting up a post at the edge of the ruined temple. After four hours Akil had come to relieve him. He'd almost sent the young boy back to his sleeping mat, knowing already sleep would be impossible.

As a child Seb had always slept as well as a hibernating bear, only rousing himself as the sunlight streamed through his bedroom window. As he got older and started to become aware of what was happening in the house around him he was plagued by sleepless nights, nights in which he'd spend long hours straining his ears to try to catch what was going on downstairs.

He'd first realised there was something not quite right between his parents when he was fourteen. At the time he'd idolised his father and had wanted to be like the stern older man in every way. Seb thought back to the night he'd discovered his father with his hands around his mother's neck. He'd been too stunned to even speak.

Shaking his head, Seb sat up. He didn't want to remember those times, he never wanted to think of his father again, but sometimes when sleep evaded him the images just kept returning.

Seb glanced into the darkness and reassured himself that Emma was still asleep. She was sleeping soundly, untroubled by the worries from the day. Even in the darkness he could make out the shape of her face and the golden locks that fell around her cheeks, framing them. Her eyelashes rested against her skin and all lines of worry that sometimes furrowed her brow in the day were smoothed by peaceful sleep.

He fought the urge to reach over and brush her hair back from her forehead, knowing any contact would be overstepping the boundaries he himself had imposed. Seb watched her sleeping for a few seconds longer, noting the tiny shiver as she shifted position and the blanket slipped from her shoulders. He stood, crossed to where she was sleeping, and readjusted the blanket, pulling it up to her chin to keep her warm. Seb stood there for a moment, fighting the urge to lie down beside her and gather her to him. If he did that he really would have to marry her.

The rebellious part of him asked whether that would really be so bad. She was beautiful and interesting and kind and—more than that—she made Seb feel truly alive. He shook his head. Any notion of marriage was just absurd. Years ago Seb had made himself a promise, one he was determined to keep. It had been made after Seb had walked in on his father punching his mother in the stomach. He'd been eighteen at the time, just back from university. He'd seen red, and had sprung to his mother's defence, coming between her and his father's fists, and after taking the blow that had been meant for his mother Seb had fought back. He'd pummelled his father so hard the older man hadn't been able to get out of bed for a week.

After that incident Seb had promised himself he would never get married. He knew he wouldn't be able to risk it. When he'd seen his father punching his mother he hadn't been able to control his response, and had had to be pulled off by three footmen. Who knew what damage he would have done if they had been alone in the house? And so Seb knew he couldn't trust himself to live intimately with a woman. He'd already shown he had a temper and a talent for violence; the last thing he wanted was to follow in his father's footsteps. The only way he could guarantee that wouldn't happen was to refrain from marriage altogether.

Over the years Seb hadn't regretted his decision once. There hadn't been any woman whom he'd pined for or lusted after enough to make him even question the logic behind his oath. But now there was Emma. She was different, unique, someone he couldn't stop thinking about. Every time she turned to him his eyes drifted towards her lips and he imagined her naked and in his bed, but it was more than just lust that consumed him. He wanted to share every new discovery and every sight with her. He loved it when her eyes lit up when he told her a story about Ancient Egypt or how she ran her fingers over the rocks that used to make up the walls of a temple.

It didn't matter, he told himself, stepping away from her sleeping form. He couldn't have her. The only way a woman of Emma's upbringing could be with him was if they married. Given what she'd already been put through by the villainous Freddie, Seb knew he couldn't ruin her reputation even further. And he wasn't prepared to marry her, no matter how much he desired her. His oath to himself was more important, and it would protect her from him in the long run. The last thing he wanted was to make her his wife, then find he was exactly like his father and subject her to a lifetime of misery.

Seb sank back down onto his own sleeping mat and turned away. His mind was made up; he couldn't marry Emma so that meant they couldn't ever be intimate. He'd just have to rein in his desire and do his job as her guide, nothing more.

As the sun started to creep up over the horizon Seb heard Emma stir. He resisted the urge to roll over and watch her as she awoke and opened her eyes for the first time, instead lying still until he was sure she was completely awake. He then made a show of stirring, as if he had slumbered peacefully the entire night.

Seb sat up and only then glanced over at Emma.

'Good morning.'

'Good morning.'

She looked delightfully tousled and Seb felt a pang of regret that after these couple of weeks together he wouldn't see her in her natural glory before she'd had a chance to attend to her toilette.

'Did you sleep well?'

Emma smiled. 'I didn't stir once between closing my eyes and waking up this morning. How about you?'

'Fine,' Seb lied. There wasn't any need for her to know he'd lain awake obsessing about her for the entire night.

Emma stood and stretched, unaware that in her sleep the shirt she was wearing had become untucked from her trousers. Seb caught a glimpse of the creamy white flesh of her abdomen as she raised her arms above her head.

'Shall I start on breakfast?' Emma asked.

Seb grunted, not trusting himself to speak. How could a sliver of skin be so enticing?

Rousing himself, Seb waited for Emma to start rummaging through their supplies before he went in search of Akins. He'd just crouched down beside the boy and was about to speak when Akins pressed a finger to his lips.

Seb scanned the horizon. The desert landscape was mainly flat, but a few hundred yards away there was a small bank. Just poking out at the top of the bank was a smudge of white looking out of place amongst the yellows and browns of the desert.

They watched in silence for five minutes. There was no movement on the bank, just the white headdress, a subtle reminder that they were being watched.

Seb motioned for Akins to follow him back to their camp. At the moment whoever was following them seemed content just to pursue them at a distance. No doubt they were waiting until they got closer to their target before making a move.

'They moved into that position about an hour before dawn,' Akins informed him.

Seb supposed their pursuers hadn't wanted to miss their departure.

'And were they taking pains to conceal themselves?'

Seb waited anxiously for Akins' answer. If their pursuers were moving in the open it meant they didn't mind Seb and his expedition knowing they were there. Somehow that made them seem more menacing.

'They were. It was only a disturbance in the dust that made me realise they were on the move.'

Seb motioned for the boy to go and have some breakfast and gently took Emma aside.

He wasn't about to scare her with talk about the fact they were being followed, but he did need to get more information out of her.

'I need to know where we're going,' Seb said.

Emma grimaced and looked down at her boots uncomfortably.

'You said when we had got started you'd give me more information. We're two days into our trek now. I need to know what direction to take next.'

Emma still didn't say anything and Seb felt all the frustrations of the last couple of days bubble up inside him.

'I'm not asking for anything extraordinary here, Emma. I'm your guide and I need to know where we're headed so I can calculate the best route.'

'I can tell you the general direction.'

Seb felt a stab of irritation that even after the last couple of days she still didn't trust him enough to share their destination.

'Not good enough,' Seb said. 'Either you show me where we are going or I'll turn back and take Akil, Akins and the horses with me.'

Emma's mouth opened in shock, then she smiled.

'You wouldn't abandon me in the middle of

the desert,' she said. 'You're too much of a gentleman for that.'

Seb cursed under his breath. She was right—there was no way his conscience would allow him to leave her unaccompanied in the desert.

'Well, I'll throw you over the front of my horse and take you right back to Cairo, then.'

He could see from the expression on her face that was a threat Emma could believe in.

For a second he hoped she wouldn't crack and tell him; he rather fancied a couple of days' trekking with Emma nestled in between his thighs.

Eventually Emma nodded but then held up a finger.

'I'm not going to show you everything,' she said.

Anything was a start.

'Wait there.'

Seb watched as she walked a few paces away from him and rummaged about in the waistband of her trousers. He wondered where exactly she was keeping this map of hers.

Impatiently he watched as she crouched down and spread out a small scroll on the ground, then strategically started covering some of it with various pebbles and items laying around their camp. After two minutes she seemed satisfied and motioned for Seb to come over.

As he neared the scroll on the ground he felt his heart start to pound in his chest. Although she had covered up most of the lower half of the scroll, which dealt with their exact destination, Emma had left the top part bare. Nestled in one corner, just as he'd caught a glimpse of in his office a few days earlier, was the seal of Rameses II. Seb didn't even have to feel the ancient papyrus to know this was the genuine article. He'd handled thousands of fakes in his time in Egypt, but this document had none of the telltale signs of a forgery.

The markings on the scroll itself were faded, and it took Seb a minute or two to decipher the curved lines and accompanying hieroglyphics. After a few minutes' perusal the picture became clearer. The scroll was a map, and surrounding the map was a detailed set of instructions on how to reach the final destination. He could now understand why Emma was so keen to go by land—the landmarks mentioned were all situated in the desert.

The bottom third of the map was covered, but Seb could work out the general direction they needed to take.

'Tonight when we stop I want you to copy out this section of the map,' he said in a tone that brooked no argument. 'Then I'll be able to guide us more accurately to all the landmarks mentioned.'

Emma nodded in agreement.

Reluctantly Seb tore his eyes away from the scroll. In itself it was a work of art, an artefact any collector or museum would pay handsomely for. He longed to know their final destination, but knew Emma wasn't ready to share that with him just yet.

'We've got a long ride,' Seb said, stepping away. 'Especially if we want to reach the winged arch before nightfall.'

The expression on Emma's face was one of glee as she looked down and picked out one of the waypoints mentioned on the map. She lovingly traced her fingers over the ancient papyrus before rolling the scroll back up and tucking it into her trousers again.

Seb boosted her onto her horse before lithely mounting his own. When he returned to Cairo it might be with the knowledge he would never see Emma again, but he had a feeling whatever they were searching for would act as some consolation for his loss.

Chapter Fifteen

⟡

Emma scanned the horizon for a distinguishing feature, something that would break up the monotonous landscape of the desert. They'd been riding for over a week and her anticipation of what was to come had reached almost breaking point. She badly wanted to reach their destination, but part of her also wanted the journey to never end. This was precious time, and once they had reached the tomb everything would change.

Emma couldn't deny she was enjoying spending time in Sebastian's company. Even after the awkwardness of their kiss she wouldn't have swapped her guide for anyone else. He made her laugh and kept her amused with his daring tales. And if she had to suppress the attraction she felt for him every time their eyes locked, surely that wasn't too great a price to pay for good company?

'Keep watching the horizon,' Sebastian said. 'Only a few minutes and Eagle rock should become visible.'

Emma didn't answer, instead resuming her scan of the desert landscape, eager to catch a glimpse of their next waypoint.

After another ten minutes Emma thought she could see something in the distance. She looked across to Sebastian, who was also staring ahead, but with a frown on his face.

He spoke rapidly in Arabic to Akil and Akins who urged their horses forward and started scanning the horizon.

'What's happening?' Emma asked, concerned by the looks on Sebastian and the boys' faces.

He didn't answer for a minute, concentrating on where the sky met the desert miles in front of them. After sixty seconds he nodded grimly.

'Sandstorm. We need to get to cover.'

Emma looked about her with concern. The desert landscape was flat and unforgiving, not providing them with much shelter at all.

'Eagle rock,' Sebastian said. 'We need to get to Eagle rock.'

Emma watched as Akil and Akins spurred

their horses forward, taking off at a canter. The beasts tossed their manes but otherwise did not protest at being urged on in the afternoon heat.

'We need to move, now.'

Emma nodded and pushed her horse forward, murmuring encouragement as she picked up speed. They covered the distance in half the time at double the speed and soon Emma could see Eagle rock protruding from the flat desert floor. In the time they had been riding Emma had become aware of the rising wall of sand in the distance, moving closer every minute. It was massive, stretching from one edge of the horizon to the other and billowing into the sky, obscuring some of the late afternoon sun.

'We should just about make it in time,' Sebastian shouted as they cantered forward.

Emma didn't bother to reply, using all her energy to keep her seat on her horse whilst watching the sandstorm power its way towards them.

After ten more minutes of riding they reached the base of Eagle rock. It was a square platform that rose from the desert floor to reach about thirty feet. At the very top there was a protrusion, carved by the wind and sand over thousands of years. Emma supposed if you squinted and used your imagination it did look a little like an eagle in flight.

As soon as they reached the rock Sebastian dismounted and quickly lifted Emma down. Akil and Akins had already started to set up their makeshift camp to shelter them from the worst of the storm.

Sebastian led their horses one by one so they were in the shelter of the rock. Calmly he coaxed them to lie down, tied them up and then tied strips of fabric across their eyes. The horses tossed their heads with fear at first but Sebastian managed to soothe them with calming words and a few strokes.

Emma looked about helplessly; she had no clue what to do. The storm was almost upon them—small particles of dust were already being whipped up into the air and the noise of the wind was almost deafening already.

After dealing with the horses Sebastian grabbed a couple of the blankets and started to secure them to the rock face in whatever way he could. Emma ran to join him and held the blankets in place whilst he tied them to each other. Slightly farther along the rock, on the other side of the horses, Emma could see Akil and Akins were doing the same.

When the blankets were secure Sebastian ushered Emma inside the makeshift tent. He followed her in a couple of minutes later holding the last of the blankets in one hand.

'We need to protect our faces,' Sebastian shouted over the noise of the sandstorm.

Emma nodded but didn't understand what to do.

'We have to wrap our shirts around our faces. It is important to cover your mouth and nose so they don't get clogged with sand.'

Emma nodded again but still didn't move.

'You're going to have to take your shirt off,' Sebastian said, slipping his over his head and starting to wrap it round his face.

Emma hesitated for only a second. Now wasn't the time to feel shy; they were in real danger. She was scared and Sebastian knew what to do to protect her.

Quickly she slipped the shirt over her head, her back to Sebastian. She felt around for the blanket he'd brought into their shelter and quickly wrapped herself in it. Then she turned around and started to try and copy what Sebastian had done with his shirt.

After a few seconds Emma felt Sebastian's fingers cover her own.

'Let me,' he said, taking the shirt from her and gently wrapping it over her mouth and nose.

Emma shuddered in anticipation. Outside the wind was howling now and the sand was battering against the exposed side of the blankets. She knew if they were out in the open the sand would tear their skin off within minutes.

After a few seconds Emma felt Sebastian slip an arm around her shoulder and ease her back against him. She stiffened at first, but then allowed herself to relax against his chest.

'In here we'll be fine,' Sebastian said. 'We just have to wait the storm out.'

'How long will it take?' Emma asked.

She felt him shrug underneath her. 'Could be a couple of hours, could be a day.'

Emma shivered at the thought of being stuck in a sandstorm for a whole day.

'Just relax, close your eyes and try and get some rest,' Sebastian said. 'We're perfectly safe in here.'

At first Emma thought the idea of rest was preposterous. She'd never been one of these people afraid of storms. In England she quite enjoyed watching the thunder and lightning pierce torrential rain from her bedroom window. But this was completely different. This was dangerous. There only needed to be a particularly strong gust of wind and their flimsy blanket shelter would be torn away and they would be exposed to the elements. Emma doubted they would survive.

The strange thing was she didn't feel particularly afraid—at least not as afraid as she should, given the circumstances. She wondered if it had something to do with Sebastian's strong arms forming a protective shield around her body. She knew he wouldn't let anything happen to her. He would throw himself on top of her to shield her from the storm if need be. Emma felt a small tingle of desire rise up inside her at the idea of Sebastian's body pressed against hers and tried to shake it off.

'Are you comfortable?' Sebastian's voice was low and close to her ear. Emma felt the small hairs on the back of her neck stand on end and wished he would lower his mouth just a little more so she could feel his lips against her skin.

'Mmm-hmm,' Emma managed to mumble.

Sebastian must have mistook her lack of eloquence for fear as he tightened his hold on her, pulling her even closer to the sculpted muscles of his chest. Emma's heart started to pound and she was convinced he must be able to feel it where their bodies met.

She squeezed her eyes tight and tried to think of anything but the man behind her. It was difficult when she felt every breath against her neck, every rise and fall of his chest through the thin blanket. Emma tried to picture something else, anything else. This was not the time to focus on her attraction to Sebastian. A very unwise attraction.

He doesn't want you, Emma told herself. That wasn't strictly true. Sebastian wanted her, she could see it in his every gesture and look, but he didn't want to marry her. He'd made that abundantly clear. Emma felt the tears well up in her eyes and was glad she was sitting with her back towards Sebastian; she didn't need him seeing her like this. It wasn't his fault men didn't find her a worthy prospect for marriage. First Freddie had rejected her, in the cruellest way possible, and now Sebastian.

Not that Sebastian was a bad man; he'd stopped himself from compromising her further because he knew he could not marry her. She should be thankful for his chivalry. But a small part of Emma was crying out, asking why men seemed to run from the idea of marrying her. Freddie she could put down to bad judgement on her part; he was a cad and a snake. Sebastian was different. He was a good man, kind and generous.

Emma sighed quietly. It was no use torturing herself. Sebastian didn't want her and she should be thankful for that. She should be grateful he would be the strong one, for it would be all too easy for her to spin around, run her fingers over his bare chest and invite him to take her.

She smiled at the thought. He'd probably back out of the makeshift tent and take his chances in the sandstorm.

Sebastian shifted a little and Emma felt herself relaxing even more into him. His arms wrapped around her were so protective and strong, and she loved the warmth emanating from his body and penetrating hers. It was no wonder she was so attracted to him. After the scandal with Freddie she'd been shunned by society. Over the years she'd been slowly accepted back into some circles, but the eligible bachelors all gave her a wide berth. Only the men with bad reputations, who made it clear they knew of her past, ever approached her, wanting to take up where Freddie had left off. No wonder she was so enamoured with Sebastian. He was a good-looking man who liked her for herself, not what he thought he could get from her.

Emma shook her head. That wasn't all of it though. If she was honest, the fact that Sebastian had been interested in her was only a small part of the attraction. He was funny and kind and generous and he had a body Emma wanted to spend all night exploring with her hands. She didn't think she'd met a more wonderful man.

It was a shame the idea of spending his life with her made him run for the hills.

Chapter Sixteen

Seb felt his head drooping as the storm started to relent outside their makeshift tent. For two hours he'd sat rigidly, holding Emma tight, hoping that their shelter would be enough to shield them from the fury of the sandstorm. The wind was still gusting outside, but it had lost its power and Seb knew that meant the worst was behind them. He'd survived many sandstorms during his time in Egypt, but only once before had he actually been caught in the desert in one. Normally the streets of Cairo would start to darken and there would be plenty of warning to get inside and cover all the windows.

The first sandstorm he'd endured in the desert had been similar to this one in many ways. It had rushed upon him with unleashed fury. That time he'd been alone and a long way from any sort of shelter. He'd wrapped his horse's upper half in a blanket, trying to shield its delicate eyes and nose from the sand, and then he'd used the second blanket to wrap himself in. For four hours he'd lain curled in a ball on the desert floor, knowing one move could dislodge the blanket and mean an agonising death.

This time had certainly been more comfortable. The shelter of the rock meant they were spared the worst of the storm and also gave them somewhere to build their makeshift tents. Sitting with his back straight, pressed against the rock, was much more preferable to spending the hours curled up in a ball. And then there was Emma. When the storm had hit he'd felt a terror like never before. Seb had always flirted with danger, never abandoning a scheme just because there was an element of risk, but never before had he felt the same terror as he had when he'd realised Emma could get injured.

Gently he tightened his grip on her and held her close, knowing the worst of the storm had passed and the danger had gone with it.

'Boys,' he called softly in Arabic.

'Boss?' Akil's voice floated back on the wind.

'Are you both well?'

He heard a giggle. 'Of course we're well.'

It took more than a sandstorm to scare the two orphans.

'Stay under cover for a few more hours,' Seb instructed.

'Yes, boss.'

Seb closed his eyes and wondered whether sleep would come. His body was relaxing now the danger had passed and he felt exhausted. The only thing preventing him from sleeping was Emma's body, moulded to his own.

It wasn't that she was heavy, or lying against him in a way that made him uncomfortable; it was more how conscious he was of their closeness. The blanket she had wrapped herself in when she'd removed her shirt had slipped from her shoulders, revealing smooth creamy skin Seb ached to touch. The thin straps of her chemise were gradually slipping lower and lower as her chest rose and fell with each breath. Seb closed his eyes and stifled a groan. This was the last thing he needed: to be stuck in a confined space with the woman he found almost irresistible and for every breath to be revealing more of her skin.

He knew he should be a gentleman, pull the blanket back into place and close his eyes, but Seb felt the stab of desire deep inside him and wondered how long he could be a gentleman for.

Without averting his eyes, he desperately tried reminding himself of all the reasons they couldn't be together. To spend a night with Emma would ruin her. It didn't matter if no one found out; it would destroy her spirit to have another man treat her like that. And Seb knew he couldn't be the one to destroy such a beautiful spirit. Equally he couldn't marry her; he wouldn't be able to live with himself if he gave in to his desires, married Emma, then his true colours came through and he hurt her as his father had hurt his mother.

Emma made a small, contented sound and burrowed even farther into his chest.

Seb couldn't help himself. He lowered his head and brushed a gentle kiss on the top of Emma's head, inhaling the sweet scent of her hair. He knew this was all he could allow himself to do, and reluctantly he pulled the blanket up so it covered Emma's shoulders and hid the temptation.

Seb must have slept although he didn't remember his eyes drooping or his muscles getting heavy. He awoke when Emma started to stir, turning against his chest so her cheek was pressed to his bare skin. Seb opened his eyes and watched her start to wake. There was a fluttering of her eyelids, a soft moan escaping from her lips, and then she was awake.

It was clear by the expressions on her face it took her a few seconds to work out where she was and the circumstances that had led them there. Seb suppressed a grin.

Suddenly her eyes widened as she looked up at Seb and realised she was burrowed into his bare chest in such an intimate fashion.

'Good morning,' Seb said, not letting his voice betray his awareness of how close they'd spent the night.

Emma sat up straight, her eyes locked on Seb's torso and her cheeks turning a soft pink colour.

'Sandstorm's passed,' Seb said conversationally.

'Oh…er…good?' Emma said, sounding more than a little flustered.

He reached for his shirt that he'd unwrapped from his face at some point in the night and slipped it back over his head. The action must have reminded Emma that she had also removed her shirt for the same purpose and that her dignity was being preserved only by a thin chemise and a strategically placed blanket. Seb watched as she grabbed the shirt and wriggled into it whilst trying to hold up the blanket with one hand.

'Ready?' Seb asked once she had got herself sorted out.

Emma nodded and they both squinted as Seb lifted the blanket up and let in the early morning sun. Quickly Seb got to his feet and offered his hand to Emma to help her up. His leg muscles were stiff after spending all night in one position and he gently stretched them out.

Akil and Akins were also just emerging from their shelter and all four of them stood for a few seconds just quietly surveying the scene.

The sky was completely clear and the sun was already beating down on the desert floor. Only their dusty camp was evidence of what had happened the previous night.

Seb went straight to the horses and started to inspect them for any injuries. His horse neighed appreciatively as he unfastened the fabric from around its eyes. Wadjet also seemed unharmed and stood almost as soon as her sight was restored.

'Boss,' Akil called to Seb quietly. 'Pharaoh is injured.'

Seb went immediately to Akil's side and started to inspect the horse. He first carefully unwrapped the animal's eyes and spent a minute soothing and stroking. Then he moved round to Pharaoh's left side where Akil was squatting. There was a deep gash in the horse's leg. At some point in the night it had stopped bleeding, but the sand was a rusty brown colour indicating the horse had lost a fair amount of blood.

Seb examined the wound, shifting slightly as he felt Emma come to his side and start stroking Pharaoh's neck, trying to comfort the injured animal. It looked as though a rock had been dislodged during the sandstorm and had fallen onto the horse's leg. Seb shuddered at the thought that just a few yards to the right and it could have hit Emma.

Carefully he eased Pharaoh to his feet and watched as the horse took a few unsteady steps.

'Boys.' Seb called the two anxious brothers over. 'Pharaoh is going to be fine,' he reassured them. Seb knew the brothers loved the horses almost as much as they loved each other. 'But he won't be able to carry anyone.'

Akil and Akins shared a glance and then grabbed one of Seb's arms each.

'We can look after him, boss,' Akil said.

'We don't need to shoot him, boss.'

Seb smiled. 'No, we don't need to shoot him.'

Emma was watching the exchange with obvious interest on her face but for the moment Seb had to organise getting Pharaoh somewhere he could be tended to.

'The best thing would be for you to take Pharaoh and Ptolemy and trek east to Luxor. Pharaoh won't be able to carry either of you, but Ptolemy is a strong horse and should manage the trip. You can lead Pharaoh.'

The brothers exchanged a few words with each other quietly.

'How long is the trek, boss?'

Seb pictured the map in his mind, identifying their current location and the location of Luxor.

'Two days, maybe three at the most. You'll be going slowly but it shouldn't take more than three.'

'What about you and the lady?' Akil asked.

Seb waited for him to continue.

'What about the people following?' he asked in a hushed whisper.

'After getting caught out in the sandstorm last night with nowhere to shelter I'm hopeful they'll have to give up and regroup.'

Akil and Akins both nodded solemnly.

'And if not I'll think of something.'

The brothers debated for a few seconds and then Akil stepped forward.

'We will take the horses to Luxor and then we will return and rejoin you.'

Seb didn't bother to question how the boys would know where to find them. He'd been impressed time and time again by their tracking skills and knew if they said they would find them then find them they would.

Quickly they started to pack up the camp. Akil and Akins only took what they needed for three days, leaving the rest of the supplies for Seb and Emma.

'What's happening?' Emma asked.

Seb spun to face her. 'The boys are taking Pharaoh back to Luxor to get his wound seen to. Then they will rejoin us.'

Emma nodded slowly, watching the brothers pack up the two horses.

'Will they be safe?'

Seb smiled. 'They lived on the streets of Cairo for years. Don't underestimate what they can do.'

'And us?' Emma asked.

'We continue.'

Emma's tongue darted out to wet her lips and Seb could see she was nervous.

'Just the two of us?'

'Just the two of us,' Seb confirmed.

Chapter Seventeen

'What will you do once this trip is over?' Sebastian asked as they rode in the afternoon sun.

Emma shrugged, not sure how to answer the question. This trip had changed everything. Even if they didn't find the tomb at the end Emma knew she would never forget this couple of weeks. She'd enjoyed a freedom she'd never known before, and she wondered whether she would ever be able to go back to the ballrooms of England and all the rules that went with them. She couldn't imagine having to have a chaperone just to talk to someone, or needing an escort if she wished to take a stroll around the park.

'I don't know,' Emma said truthfully. 'I'm not sure I can return to my normal life.'

'Egypt's captured your heart,' Sebastian said softly. 'It was the same for me. I didn't plan on staying, in fact I hadn't planned on settling anywhere, but when I first sailed down the Nile into Cairo I knew I wouldn't be able to leave.'

'It is a captivating country,' Emma said, 'but it's more than that.'

She wondered how to explain exactly how she felt to Sebastian. He was a man; he had freedom and the choice to do whatever he wanted, whenever he wanted. He didn't need to be accompanied everywhere by an unmarried aunt, and if he got caught up in a scandal it would probably enhance his reputation, not ruin it.

'I love Egypt,' Emma said. 'I think I've loved it all my life—my father's stories made me desperate to visit. But it's more than that. In England I'm a prisoner.' Emma paused as she saw the expression on Sebastian's face. 'At least it feels as though I am.'

'You're not free to do what you want?'

'There are so many rules and conventions. And if you break one, even just a little, you become an outcast, an outsider.'

'Whereas here in Egypt you're free to be yourself and do what you want?'

Emma nodded, pleased he understood.

'It would be hard to go back to your life in England after enjoying this freedom,' Sebastian said.

Emma sighed. She knew that. Often during the quiet hours of the afternoon as they were riding through the desert she wondered what she would do. If she were a man she would set herself up in business in Cairo, translating old manuscripts and living off her inheritance. But for a woman it wouldn't be that simple. Even here, in such an exotic country, there were still the same rules when you scratched the surface. No one would take their business to an unmarried woman who lived on her own, and she wouldn't fit into any aspect of society—she'd be lonely.

'It would be very hard, but I don't have much choice. I can't very well live here on my own.'

They rode on in silence for a few minutes and Emma began wishing their trip could last for ever. This was where she was happiest, in the desert on an adventure with Sebastian by her side.

'We should reach the sunken oasis in about an hour,' Sebastian said, breaking the silence.

This brought a smile to Emma's face. It was well over a week since they'd stopped the first night in the oasis, but Emma could still close her eyes and imagine its beauty in intricate detail.

'Don't expect too much,' Sebastian said. 'I

travelled this way a few years ago and there was little more than a muddy puddle left.'

It didn't matter, not really. She would have liked to ease into the water and wash some of the dust from her hair and body, but in reality she didn't mind if they camped near the most beautiful oasis or on a dried river bed. After a hard day's riding she was always thankful to rest her head and close her eyes and sleep was never far behind.

After a couple more hours they arrived at the oasis and Emma could see Sebastian was right. There were signs the spot had once been teeming with life; more scrubby bushes than elsewhere in the desert and deep dips and banks that signified the flow of water. In the centre were a few dead trees and a tiny circle of clear water.

'At least it's clean,' Sebastian said, regarding the oasis with a critical eye. 'We'll be able to refill our water skins.'

After refilling the dozen water skins they carried Emma doubted there would be anything left of the oasis.

'And we can have a fire. There's plenty of wood.'

He was right. Which meant hot food. Emma hadn't minded surviving on dried bread, dried fruit and dried meats, but now she craved something different, something cooked.

Efficiently they started to set up their camp. It seemed quiet without Akil and Akins bustling round, but they soon had everything sorted for the night. The sun was dipping in the sky and Emma knew darkness was just minutes away.

'Shall I gather some firewood?' she asked.

Sebastian nodded, keeping one eye on the horizon.

'Good idea. Ten minutes and we won't be able to see anything.'

Quickly Emma gathered an armful of twigs and sticks, all dry and brittle from baking in the sun. Masterfully Sebastian coaxed a tiny flame into a flickering fire.

After a few minutes they sat back and regarded the fire. It would certainly do for cooking and should also keep them warm for a good few hours into the night.

'Shall I go and fetch some water?' Emma asked, wondering what Sebastian would produce from his bag for dinner.

Sebastian nodded, already rummaging and pulling out the cooking pots. 'Be careful,' he warned. 'It'll be pitch black in a minute and you won't be able to see where you're going.'

Emma carefully picked her way over the scrubby bushes towards the oasis. She started to fill an empty water skin when a rustle behind her startled her so much she almost overbalanced. Telling herself it was probably nothing more than her imagination, Emma stood and looked into the darkness. She watched for thirty seconds and was just about to turn around again when something moved. Emma felt her heart start to pound in her chest and her throat went dry. She peered into the blackness and wondered what it was. She knew there were some dangerous animals in the desert, but most were small and wouldn't make this much noise.

Swallowing nervously, she glanced towards the flicker of the fire and wondered if she could call out for Sebastian. She still couldn't see what was making the noise, but he would know what to do, and more importantly he would be able to protect her if it was something larger and more sinister.

Emma thought back to the day in Cairo when she'd returned to find the menacing man in her room. Surely he wouldn't have followed her all this way, and if he had surely he would have made his move before now?

Her breathing shallow and panicky, Emma

started to back away from the spot the noise had come from. Her eyes were fixed to the darkness as she wondered if she would detect any attack before it came.

Suddenly Emma felt her foot connect with a long-dead tree root, which pushed her off balance. Frantically she flailed about with her arms, trying to keep upright, but she knew it was no use. Letting out a short, sharp shout, Emma toppled backwards and fell onto her backside.

Sebastian was at her side within seconds.

'What happened?' he asked when he saw her siting inelegantly on the ground. 'Are you hurt?'

Emma shook her head. 'I heard a noise, over there.' She pointed to the darkness and watched as Sebastian strode forward. He was silent for a few seconds then he chuckled.

'What?' Emma asked.

'It's just a bird,' he said. 'It looks like a kite.'

Emma immediately felt foolish. She'd been imagining an armed assailant and it was just a bird.

Sebastian strode back over to her and held out a hand to help her up. Emma took it and started to pull herself to her feet. A red-hot stab of pain burst through her ankle and she fell back with a cry. Immediately Sebastian was kneeling in front of her, concern etched on his face.

'What is it?' he asked.

'My ankle.' Emma gritted her teeth as the pain started to subside now she wasn't putting any weight on it.

Sebastian started to pull at the laces of her boots, but in the darkness the knots were too much and Emma heard him curse under his breath. With no warning he stood, leant over and picked Emma up in his arms. She felt her heart pound as he carried her gently back towards the fire. It seemed as if he was exerting almost no effort at all, and Emma realised she liked the feel of his arms looped under her back and his chest pressed against her body.

He lowered her to the ground in front of the fire and then knelt at her feet. With the light of the fire now illuminating everything, Sebastian quickly undid her laces and pulled the boot from her foot. Emma grimaced as a bolt of pain shot through her and tried not to let the tears that were welling up in her eyes fall.

With a feather-light touch Sebastian inspected her ankle. Even from her position Emma could see it had started to swell. Expertly Sebastian pressed at different points over her skin and watched her expression. As he got to an area just below her ankle bone Emma let out a muffled scream.

'Good,' Sebastian said, satisfied.

'Good?' Emma couldn't help but sound indignant. How could her pain be good?

'It's not broken.'

It felt as though it were broken.

'You've sprained it, but it'll heal.'

'Will I be able to walk?' Emma asked.

Sebastian nodded. 'But it'll hurt the first few days.'

'We don't have to go back?'

He grinned and Emma found herself smiling back. 'We don't have to go back.'

Emma looked again at the ankle and surveyed the damage. When she kept it completely still it wasn't too painful. The agony came with just the slightest of movement.

'You'll still be able to ride,' Sebastian said, 'and you'll just have to rest it of an evening.'

He moved away and started to gather a few things, bringing them to her after a couple of minutes.

'I'm going to bind your ankle,' he said. 'Ideally this should be ice, but water's the best we've got.'

Emma watched as he dipped strips of torn fabric into a bowl of water and gently but firmly started to bind her ankle.

'It's fine to cry,' Sebastian said as he watched her bite her lip.

Emma felt the tears spill down her cheeks and every so often she would let out a moan of pain. Sebastian murmured soothingly, but never once did he stop binding. After a few minutes he sat back and surveyed his work.

Emma had to admit it did feel better already. The water was cool against her skin and the fabric felt as if it was holding everything in place.

'Hopefully it will stop some swelling and we'll be able to get your boot on tomorrow.'

He checked one last time the bindings wouldn't come loose then he came and sat by Emma's side.

'Hush,' he said softly, reaching up and wiping a tear from Emma's cheek. 'It'll feel better in the morning.'

As he leant in closer towards her Emma forgot about the pain in her ankle, and she forgot the terror she'd felt when she'd heard the rustle in the darkness. She forgot her determination not to kiss Sebastian again and the hurt after his rejection the last time. Her mind emptied and all she could think about was Sebastian's lips meeting her own.

Slowly they came together. The kiss was gentle and unhurried. As Sebastian brushed his lips against hers Emma felt her body relax against his and she wished they could remain sealed together all night.

Chapter Eighteen

'Oh, Emma,' Seb heard himself murmur as he pulled away from her lips to brush kisses along her neck. She moaned and shuddered under his touch and Seb knew what he was doing was wrong, but he couldn't seem to stop. He was driven by a primal lust that had taken over his body and silenced the voice of reason in his head.

Slowly Seb felt his hand start to caress Emma's back. He trailed his fingers through the loose strands of hair at her neck, traced a pattern over the soft skin at her nape and then let his hand drop to her back where he used it to pull her closer to him.

Just as he felt the arousal spread through his body Emma gently pulled away. She looked deep into his eyes and Seb fought to meet such an intense gaze.

'We shouldn't be doing this,' Emma said breathlessly.

Seb couldn't say anything. He knew they shouldn't be doing this, every part of him knew what they were doing was wrong, but he wanted it so badly. He wanted her so badly.

'You can't marry me,' Emma said, her voice flat, 'and I can't lose my head over a man who won't marry me. At least not again,' she murmured.

Seb found himself nodding even though he desperately wanted to scream in protest.

Emma shifted slightly, pulling herself farther away. She had wrapped her arms around her body in a protective manner and as he watched, Seb could see her withdrawing into herself, into a little protective shell. He wanted to reach out and stop her, to pull her back into his arms.

'Emma, if I could marry anyone it would be you,' Seb said softly.

She snorted and tears started to well in her eyes.

'It would be you. You're beautiful and kind and interesting. I'm never bored when I'm with you. You'd make anyone a wonderful wife.'

'Just not wonderful enough for you.'

He didn't know how to reply. Seb reached out

and took her hands in his own, wincing as she pulled away. Determinedly he caught her fingers and gripped them tightly.

She looked beautiful in the light of the fire. The glow from the flickering flames made her hair shine like strands of gold and her complexion looked rosy. Seb wondered when she had started to mean so much to him. The idea of losing her, even just emotionally, was like a punch in the gut. He knew life without her would seem empty, pointless, and he'd only known her a couple of weeks.

He couldn't bear the thought that he was the one hurting her. He needed her to understand, to look at him with something other than hurt in her eyes.

'I need to tell you something,' Seb said, sitting back but not letting go of Emma's hand.

She turned to him and for a long moment Seb thought she might turn away and leave him aching for her.

'What do you need to tell me?' she asked eventually.

He took his time to collect his thoughts, knowing he only had one chance to make her understand, or he would lose her for good. Seb had never told anyone about his past before, and he knew it would be difficult to put into words something he tried to block from his memories.

'When I was a child I thought my parents were happy,' he started. 'My father would kiss my mother's cheek every morning, and he would buy her lavish gifts on her birthday or at Christmas. Sometimes even for no reason at all.'

Seb paused, wondering how best to describe the atmosphere in his childhood home. It was only something he had been aware of looking back; as a child he had been oblivious to some of the frostiness.

'Looking back I now see it wasn't a happy home, but as a child I just couldn't see the truth. I thought it was normal for my mother to hardly speak, to shrink slightly when her husband entered the room.'

He stared into the distance, trying to stop the pull of the memories from taking him back to the house in England.

'She was scared of him,' Emma said softly.

Seb nodded. 'I see that now, but as a child I had no idea.'

He'd often wondered whether things might have been different if he'd noticed his mother wasn't happy, if he would have been able to do something if only he'd known. He'd spent hours torturing himself in this way, even though it was all in the past.

'On the few occasions I can remember being alone with my mother, if my father had to rush to London for business, she was completely different. It was as though she came alive.'

Emma squeezed his hand supportively and Seb started to feel the catharsis of telling someone his story after all these years.

'She would laugh, and play the piano and chase me around the garden. Then my father would return and she would retreat back into herself.'

As a child he had always wondered why his mother seemed to have two sides to her character, but he'd never even suspected his father was the cause.

'I was sent away to school when I was thirteen and, looking back, I think that only made things worse. When I returned for the holidays I started to notice my mother would always wear long-sleeved, high-necked dresses, as if she were trying to cover something up.'

'Bruises and injuries?' Emma asked.

Seb shook his head, wishing that his younger self had realised earlier what had been going on in his very own home. Maybe then he would have been able to do something sooner.

'Sebastian, you were just a child,' Emma said softly. He felt a shiver run down the length of his spine as she used his name. It sounded silky and exotic on her lips.

'I was just a child, but a damn blind one. I didn't see for fourteen years that my father beat my mother.'

'What happened?'

'I was home from school for Christmas. It was late at night but I just couldn't sleep so I decided to get up and choose a book from the library.' He could still remember the walk through the chilly corridors as if it were yesterday. 'The house was quiet, but as I neared the library I could see there was a light coming from under the door. I nearly turned back, not wanting to get into trouble for being out of bed so late at night.'

He paused and relived the seconds of indecision in the cold hallway. His mind had been made up to return to bed when he heard a rasping noise. His curiosity had won out.

'I pushed open the library door, just an inch, just enough to see through, and peered inside.'

Seb felt Emma's grip on his hand tighten as she willed him to go on with his story.

'What did you see?'

He swallowed. The image was one he'd never been able to rid himself of, one that popped up in his mind every so often to remind him where he came from.

'My father's hands were around my mother's throat and he was choking her.' Seb stared into the fire, hoping the flicker of the flames would wipe the memory.

Emma gasped and pulled herself closer to him. Seb barely noticed; he was aged fourteen again, angry and confused and unsure what to do.

'What did you do?' Emma asked.

Seb laughed, but it was a strained, unnatural sound.

'Not enough,' he said, his voice hard with emotion.

He should have done more, that was what he'd always felt, then maybe his father would have stopped beating his mother, maybe she would still be alive today.

'I pushed the door open fully and the sound of it banging against a bookshelf was enough to make my father pause.' He still remembered the look of guilt on his father's face as his son had caught him strangling the woman he was supposed to protect and cherish.

'Like all bullies he didn't want a confrontation. He let go of my mother and came straight to me.'

'Did he hurt you?'

Seb shook his head ruefully. 'His precious son and heir, the boy who was meant to carry on the family name?'

His father had led him from the room, put distance between him and his mother.

'He said that he and Mother were having an argument and that everything was fine.'

Seb could still see the flash of desperation in the old man's eyes as he'd tried to hide his true character from his son.

'My mother followed us after a few minutes, hugged me, and told me it was just a misunderstanding.'

'She said that?'

Seb nodded. He'd been shaken, distressed, but when his mother had emerged from the library looking composed his doubts had eased.

'I believed her. At the time I couldn't understand why she would lie. And it was easier to believe them both than to have to reassess my whole world, my whole life.'

Emma squeezed his hand, pulling him back to the present.

'You were only a child,' she said again. 'You had no reason to believe your mother was lying.'

Seb barked a harsh laugh. 'I was fourteen, plenty old enough to realise what was really going on.'

'As children we are programmed to see the best in our parents. They are our heroes. When something happens to shatter that, it is only natural to want to hold onto the illusion.'

Seb sat back and ran a hand through his hair. For years he'd wondered why his mother had protected his father, why she had pretended everything was fine when it wasn't. Then he'd accepted the simple truth: it had all been for him. To give him a pleasant home life, to shield him from his father's tempers. She had borne her suffering in silence so he would grow up in an environment that at least seemed happy.

'For months I dreamt of my father's hands around my mother's neck. I couldn't quite forget the image, and then suddenly it was gone.'

He glanced up at Emma and knew that as yet she didn't understand, that at the moment she pitied him and his childhood. Seb hadn't told this story for pity; he had to make her see what he was really like, what he could turn into.

'I went back to school and gradually I forgot, or at least I suppressed the memory. Every holiday it became easier to come home and eventually I stopped wondering if I would walk in on something untoward. I accepted the incident had been a one-off.'

'You can't blame yourself for moving on,' Emma said softly.

He did though. He blamed himself for not looking harder, for not wanting to know for sure.

'When I was eighteen I went off to Cambridge. We were let off our studies a couple of days early and I thought I'd surprise my parents by arriving home early for Christmas.'

He'd been exuberant on the journey home, bursting to tell his parents stories of his first term at Cambridge.

'When I got home the house was quiet. There were no servants downstairs to greet me. I thought it odd, but didn't realise the implications.'

Seb felt Emma's grip on his hand tighten as she realised he was getting to the crux of his tale.

'I heard a noise, just a faint sobbing sound, and immediately I knew it was my mother.'

Seb could remember running up the stairs, taking them three at a time, dreading what he would find when he was at the top.

'I burst into my mother's bedroom. It was the first time in years that I'd been inside. And there he was, punching her over and over again in the stomach.'

Seb felt the bile rise in his throat as he relived the moment he'd seen his father beat his mother so viciously. Emma had gone completely still beside him.

'He didn't realise I was there at first, and he just kept punching her, telling her what a useless woman she was.'

His mother had been facing him and her eyes had locked with his and silently she'd begged him to leave.

'I saw red. I couldn't control myself. I pulled my father away from her and before he knew what was happening I was pummelling him. I hit him for all the years of misery he must have put my mother through.' Seb took a deep breath. 'I nearly killed him, Emma. I couldn't stop myself. I wanted him to hurt like he'd made her hurt. I wanted him to bleed.'

He took a couple of deep breaths and continued. 'A footman heard the commotion and pulled me off him. It took three of them to finally restrain me.'

By that point his father had been a bloody mess, his features nearly indistinguishable.

'He was in bed for a week. During that time I begged my mother to leave him. Promised her I would take care of her, but she wouldn't, she stayed by his side.'

'What did you do?' Emma asked.

'I was so angry with them both. I hated him but I was angry with my mother for not leaving him.'

Emma nodded as if sensing there was something he hadn't told her yet.

'When my father began to recover I refused to stay in the same house as him. I took a room in the inn in the village and went to visit my mother every day. Every day I begged her to leave him.'

'But she wouldn't.'

Seb shook his head. 'My father largely stayed out of my way, but he was always there in the background, watching us, wielding his power over my mother.'

He swallowed as he felt the lump start to form in his throat.

'I was due to go back to Cambridge, but I knew I couldn't leave my mother. I worried what my father would do to her if I wasn't around.'

Emma squeezed his hand and encouraged him to continue.

'Not that my presence did much good.' Seb felt the tears build in his eyes and blinked them away. 'One afternoon I went up to the house. Just as I was waiting to see my mother, to try one last time to convince her to leave, I heard raised voices. My father was shouting at her.'

Seb took a deep breath and tried to continue. 'Then I heard an awful crash. I came running out into the hall to find my mother at the bottom of the stairs. She wasn't moving.'

Emma moved in closer to him, but Seb hardly noticed. He was back in his ancestral home, looking down at his mother's unseeing eyes.

'My father was just standing at the top of the stairs, not moving.'

'Did he…?' Emma's words trailed off.

Seb didn't know how to answer because he didn't know. 'Did he push her? I don't know. He told everyone she wasn't concentrating and she slipped. It could be the truth, but, if he was capable of beating her, he was certainly capable of pushing her down the stairs.'

'What did you do?' Emma asked.

'I left. After the funeral I knew I couldn't stay anywhere near my father. I left home and I left England and eventually I left Europe. I never saw my father again.'

There was silence as Seb tried to separate himself from the memories and Emma struggled to take in what he'd told her.

'So you see,' he said eventually, 'that's why I can't ever marry.'

Chapter Nineteen

Emma frowned. Sebastian's tale was awful, there was no denying that, but she still didn't quite understand why his past, and in particular his father, meant he couldn't get married.

'You do know you are not the same man as your father?' Emma asked softly.

Sebastian shook his head. 'I'm capable of great violence, Emma. I nearly killed my father.'

'For beating your mother. You were protecting her.'

Sebastian shook his head again. 'It doesn't matter. I have that same rage inside me.'

Emma stroked the back of his hand softly with her thumb. She could see the anguish in his eyes and wished she could take away all the pain and guilt.

'You did what any good man would do. You

defended your mother against someone who was hurting her.'

Sebastian turned towards her and Emma nearly gasped at the emptiness in his eyes. It was as though his soul had been ripped from his body.

'I saw red, Emma—when I walked in and he was punching her, I couldn't control my actions.'

Emma nodded, knowing there was more to come.

'My father has written to me many times since I left England, but it was his first letter that chilled me to the bone.' He took a deep breath and stared into the distance. 'He tried to explain why he did what he did. His excuse? "Sometimes he saw red."'

Emma didn't know what to say. Somehow she had to get across that Sebastian wasn't the same man as his father, that just because he'd experienced uncontrollable rage towards the man who was beating his mother, that didn't mean he in turn would hurt an innocent woman. She could see he was drowning in guilt and worry about what kind of man he might be.

'Sebastian,' Emma said gently, waiting for him to meet her eye before continuing, 'you are one of the finest men I've ever known. You are good and honest and true. You can't run from life just because of an unsubstantiated worry that you might have some of your father in you.'

'I can't risk it,' Sebastian said, his voice hoarse. 'If I were to…' He trailed off. 'If we were to marry and then I hurt you, I couldn't live with myself. And I can't take the risk of hurting someone who means so much to me.'

Emma's heart swelled inside her chest. She had known he was attracted to her, that much was obvious from their multiple kisses, but she hadn't been sure if his feelings ran any deeper. Now she knew; he cared for her. He hadn't said he loved her, but he cared for her and that made her head spin and her heart soar.

'You can't live your whole life in the shadows, missing out on what's important, just because of a fear of what you might be.'

Sebastian shook his head. 'That's better than turning into a man like my father.'

'You're stronger than that, Sebastian.' She reached up and brushed her fingers across his cheek. 'I believe in you. I believe you would be able to control yourself if the anger started to creep up.'

He looked deep into her eyes for a long minute and Emma knew he was battling with himself. She could tell he wanted to believe her, that he wanted to give himself permission to do all the things that he had been so far denied.

Emma shuffled closer to him, careful to keep her ankle completely still. Her body was aching with longing for this man. She wanted to cover his lips with her own and make the years of pain and guilt disappear.

She hesitated. It was one thing being a good friend to him, to convince him to live his life to the full and believe he was a good person, but Emma knew she wanted much more than that. She wanted to feel the heat of his body as he pressed up against her and she wanted to feel the caress of his lips over her skin.

She knew it would be a bad idea—past experience had shown her that—but Sebastian was different. She knew he wouldn't abandon her in the middle of the night. He might not want to marry her, but he was a good man; he wouldn't leave her alone to fend for herself.

Emma wondered if she was just fooling herself. After Freddie she had vowed never to let another man come close to her, a vow that hadn't been difficult to keep because she hadn't desired anyone. Until now. Maybe that desire was clouding her judgement.

Emma raised her hand again and tentatively ran a finger over Sebastian's jaw. Far from the clean-shaven man she had first met in Cairo, Sebastian now had a thick beard, which he kept trimmed close to his face.

Their eyes locked together and Emma knew she was lost. It might be a bad idea and it might be against every promise she'd made to herself, but she knew soon she wouldn't be able to stop. One kiss from Sebastian's lips and she would be lost.

Slowly Sebastian dipped his head and moved towards her. Emma held her breath in anticipation of his lips meeting hers. The kiss started out soft, a gentle brush of his lips against hers, but Emma knew she needed more.

Her fingers snaked through his hair and pulled him more firmly against her, the kiss quickly turning from tentative to passionate. Sebastian looped his arm around her back and gently laid her down on the blanket spread beneath them.

Emma gasped as his lips left hers and started to trail across her jaw and down her neck. She shuddered with pleasure as he nibbled on her earlobe and drew his lips over the soft skin of her cheek. And then suddenly his mouth was back on hers and he kissed her with such an intensity Emma almost forgot to breathe. She gasped as she felt his tongue dart between her lips and join with hers and she felt her hips instinctively rise to meet his.

All too soon he pulled away, holding himself just inches above her. Emma froze, wondering whether he was going to stop completely, wondering if she would actually scream with frustration if he did.

'I want to see you,' he whispered, his voice hoarse.

Emma nodded, but didn't move, unsure exactly what he wanted her to do.

Gently Sebastian started pulling Emma's shirt out of the waistband of her trousers. She shivered as his fingers brushed against the thin cotton of the chemise covering her abdomen and she felt her whole body tighten in anticipation. Slowly he lifted the shirt up, and Emma obligingly raised her head so he could slip it off.

Even though she was still clad in her chemise and trousers Emma felt rather exposed. No one had ever looked at her the way Sebastian was looking at her. It was as though he wanted to devour her with his eyes.

Sebastian began caressing her abdomen with

the palm of his hand, the warmth of his skin easily penetrating her thin chemise.

'You next,' Emma said breathlessly, causing him to pause a second, then chuckle.

'I suppose it's only fair,' he said eventually as he slipped his shirt over his head.

Emma had seen Sebastian's naked torso before, when she had peeked whilst he exited the oasis, but this time he was so much closer. Tentatively she raised her hand and raked her fingers over his skin. Sebastian let his head arch back and groaned.

Suddenly he dipped and caught her mouth with his own, his body pressing against hers. Emma relished the warmth of his skin penetrating the thin cotton of her chemise and wondered what it would feel like if her bare skin were pressed against his.

She didn't have to wonder for long. After a minute Sebastian broke off the kiss and gripped the bottom of Emma's chemise.

'I need to see you,' he said again, his voice thick and gravelly.

Emma nodded, not trusting herself to speak.

Torturously slowly Sebastian lifted her chemise so it exposed her stomach. He paused just before he reached her breasts, glancing at Emma before continuing.

As her skin was bared to the night air Emma felt it start to tighten. She felt the buds of her nipples harden in response to Sebastian's gaze and unconsciously she arched her back up, urging him to touch her.

It was far from the gentle caress she'd imagined; Emma almost squealed as Sebastian lowered his head to take one nipple into his mouth. She writhed as he flicked and sucked and she let out a low moan of pleasure mixed with desire.

Without lifting his mouth from her skin, Sebastian trailed kisses across the valley between her breasts and caught the other nipple in his mouth. Emma wondered if she would explode from the sheer pleasure of it. She felt her hips bucking upwards instinctively and she let her hands trail through Sebastian's hair, urging him to continue with his sensual assault.

All too soon he broke off the contact and lifted himself so he was once again a few inches above her.

'Where were we?' he asked.

'You were…er…' Emma trailed off as she felt the first flood of blood to her cheeks.

'Ah, yes, we were helping you to undress.'

Emma caught his hand as he reached for the waistband of her trousers.

'It's your turn.'

He grinned, then kicked off his boots and socks.

Emma frowned.

'That's hardly fair,' she said. 'My boots had to come off earlier.'

'I'll make it up to you.'

Emma was about to protest further when he lowered his lips to her skin and started to pepper kisses across her abdomen. As his mouth dipped even lower she shuddered in anticipation. Gently Sebastian hooked one hand into the waistband of her trousers and ran his finger across her hidden skin.

Emma froze, realising the scroll was tucked into her waistband. She knew when Sebastian's fingers came upon it and she watched as slowly he plucked the ancient papyrus from her trousers and carefully placed it into the bag at her side. Then his attention was focussed once again entirely on her.

'Your turn,' he said.

Emma felt her hips pushing up towards him as he quickly unfastened the belt and buttons holding her trousers up. She obligingly lifted her bottom from the ground as Sebastian tugged the trousers down and discarded them over his shoulders.

Emma knew the intensity of Sebastian's gaze as his eyes travelled down her body should make her want to cover up. Here she was lying naked underneath him, spread out brazenly, and instead of feeling ashamed she felt empowered. She loved the desire in his eyes as he perused her body and she loved the reaction she elicited from him.

'You're beautiful,' Sebastian said simply.

Emma felt the tears flood to her eyes. She could see he meant it. It wasn't a meaningless compliment from a man more interested in her inheritance than in her. And it wasn't flattery designed to get her into bed. Here she was, already resolved to give herself to Sebastian and he was telling her how beautiful she was.

She blinked the tears away and gasped as Sebastian ran his fingers across her lower abdomen. His gaze was fixed somewhat lower and Emma knew it was only a matter of time before he touched her there. Ever so slowly he trailed backwards and forward across her skin. Emma felt herself writhe and buck under his touch and even though she knew it was wanton she just wanted his fingers to graze over her most private of places.

'Patience, my love,' Sebastian said with a grin. 'We'll get there in good time.'

'Isn't it your turn to undress?' Emma asked, her breathing laboured as she struggled to control her desire.

'Soon.'

Emma felt her hips buck as Sebastian's finger dipped lower and rested on her silky folds. He paused a second, then Emma gasped as he dipped inside her.

Her eyes were wide open with shock as he continued to caress and stroke her, working her up into a frenzy. She heard a guttural moan and realised the sound had escaped from her own lips. Emma's hips started to thrust in time to his fingers and as he caressed and massaged her most sensitive area Emma felt a tightening deep inside her.

Sebastian slowly increased the pace and Emma felt a tingling spreading all over her body. She writhed beneath his touch, simultaneously begging him to go faster, deeper and pleading for him to stop. She didn't know if she could take much more pleasure.

Suddenly Emma felt her whole world stop.

The tightening inside exploded and waves of pleasure spread through her body. She tried to grip the ground with her fingers and felt her toes curl on the ends of her feet. A scream of pleasure exploded from deep within her throat and for an eternity it felt as though she were floating.

After a while Emma started to regain her senses. She pushed herself up on her elbows and looked at Sebastian, her eyes wide.

'What was that?' she asked, her voice shaky.

Sebastian grinned. 'Did you enjoy it?'

'I don't think "enjoy" is a strong enough word,' she said eventually.

Sebastian leant over her and gently kissed her on the lips.

'You deserve to be cherished and pleasured every day of your life,' he murmured in her ear.

'I don't know if I can cope with that amount of pleasure every day.'

Sebastian grinned again. 'How about twice in an hour?'

Emma's eyes widened and slowly her gaze dropped to the visible bulge in Sebastian's trousers. Slowly, without moving her eyes, she reached out and fumbled with his waistband.

Chapter Twenty

Seb groaned as Emma's fingers fumbled with his waistband. She was beautiful, lying beneath him looking just the slightest bit dishevelled. He resisted the urge to rip his trousers down himself, knowing the anticipation would only make things better.

Eventually Emma unfastened enough of the buttons to pull his trousers down over his hips. Seb quickly pulled them all the way off then paused as he caught the look in Emma's eyes.

'It won't fit,' she said.

Seb chuckled. 'Thank you for the compliment, but I can assure you it will fit.'

Emma shook her head in disbelief.

Knowing he still had to be gentle with her, even though this wasn't technically her first time, Seb lowered his head and covered her mouth with his own. Softly he kissed her, tracing her lower lip with his tongue and gently catching it between his teeth. Slowly Emma started to writhe beneath him again, unconsciously thrusting her hips up to meet his.

He could feel his hardness pressing against her and ached to be buried deep inside her, but Seb knew Emma deserved more than that. She deserved passion and gentle lovemaking. And he was determined to give her something she would remember for ever, something to wipe away the pain that lowlife had caused her when he'd abandoned her all those years ago.

'Sebastian.' Emma moaned his name in his ear. He didn't know if it was an entreaty for more or just a moan of pleasure.

He dipped his head and peppered kisses over her breasts, capturing one nipple in his mouth and teasing it with his tongue until Emma begged for mercy. She was thrusting her hips up to meet his with such rhythm and force now Seb knew he couldn't wait any longer. He wanted her, but more than that he needed her.

Gently he pulled away and looked into Emma's eyes.

'This might hurt,' he said quietly.

He felt her tense underneath him, her hips freezing mid thrust; a look of panic flooded into her eyes.

Silently Seb cursed Freddie the lowlife for giving her such a bad experience. Emma was a passionate woman, but here she was frozen at the idea of him entering her.

Seb looked deep into her eyes and knew he had to fix this. He had to show her not all men were like her ex-fiancé.

'Relax, my love,' he said as he lowered his head again to kiss her. Slowly, as his lips caressed hers, Seb felt her muscles relax underneath him. Ever so gently he pushed forward, distracting her with kisses. This time when she clenched it was only momentary and Seb gently entered farther.

A small moan emanated from Emma's lips and Seb couldn't help but smile. Her eyes had glazed over and her breathing had become more laboured. As he pushed farther inside her he felt her hips rise to meet his.

He tried to control himself, knowing this had to be special for Emma, but his desire nearly overtook him. Slowly he pulled back so he had nearly pulled out of her. He felt Emma's hands on his buttocks, holding him in place.

'I'm not going anywhere,' he assured her.

As he thrust back in he looked deep into Emma's eyes and he knew this moment would stay with him for ever. She was special, this woman of his, and he knew he was losing his heart to her.

Emma met each of his thrusts with increasing vigour and Seb knew he couldn't last much longer. Faster and faster they moved together and suddenly Emma's whole body arched and her muscles clenched against him. It was enough to send Seb over the edge and he felt the exquisite release.

Breathing heavily, Seb held himself above Emma and looked down at her face. Her eyes were still closed but a faint smile darted over her lips. She looked contented.

Gently he pulled out of her and lay down beside her, gathering her petite body to his chest. He pressed his torso against her back and felt his breathing synchronise with the rise and fall of her chest.

'Sebastian…' Emma murmured. 'You're very good at that.'

Seb grinned. 'Just what a man wants to hear from his woman,' he whispered in her ear.

Gently he kissed the nape of her neck and held her tight against him, wondering if he would ever be able to let this wonderful woman go.

Chapter Twenty-One

Emma woke slowly. She had a wonderful feeling of contentment deep inside and for a few seconds she allowed herself to bask in it. She stretched and eventually allowed her eyes to flutter open.

The sun was just rising above the horizon and the chill of the night was still in the air. Shivering, she pulled the blanket Sebastian must have laid over her to cover up her shoulders.

Lazily she rolled over. Then she frowned. She'd assumed Sebastian would still be behind her. She could remember him pulling her body tight against his before she fell asleep and she'd thought he'd still be somewhere close by.

Slowly Emma sat up and looked around. There was just enough light to make out the surroundings and she took her time trying to make out Sebastian's form in the dried-up oasis.

'Sebastian?' she called softly, wondering if he had gone to fetch something to get started on breakfast. She was ravenous and wouldn't mind having something to still the growling in her belly.

'Sebastian?' she called a little louder, knowing they were the only two probably within a hundred miles.

No answer. With a frown Emma reached for her clothes where they had discarded them the night before. She shook out the shirt, knowing the creases would never fall out after it had spent a night in a crumpled pile. Quickly she pulled on her chemise and shirt, then the trousers. She stood to tuck her top half into the waistband of the trousers.

Knowing she must look an absolute state, Emma was glad there wasn't a mirror around to confirm her suspicions. She quickly redid her hair, all the time scanning the surroundings, hoping for a glimpse of Sebastian.

Emma slowly started to pick her way through the scrubby undergrowth, wincing with every step she took on her swollen ankle. She gritted her teeth and continued; at least she could walk on it even if it did hurt.

When she had covered half the perimeter

of the dried-up oasis Emma began to panic. Where on earth was Sebastian? She imagined him fallen into a gorge or bitten by a poisonous animal.

Then she reached the spot where they'd tethered the horses.

Wadjet was standing quietly, waiting for the day to start. Emma absent-mindedly patted the horse on the neck as she looked around. Sebastian's horse was nowhere to be seen. There were hoof marks and half-chewed bits of vegetation, but no horse.

With a horrible sinking feeling in her stomach Emma hobbled back to the camp as quickly as possible. Surely he wouldn't have left her? Surely she hadn't misjudged him quite so badly?

She was almost sobbing by the time she had returned to where they had slept after making love only a few hours before. She fell to her knees and frantically started searching through the bag she'd kept by her side their whole journey. The bag Sebastian had placed the scroll into last night.

Frantically she searched through the bag, hoping the ancient scroll was still there, unwilling to think the worst of Sebastian just yet.

Eventually she emptied the entire contents

of the bag onto the ground. When they were spread out with nowhere to hide, it was obvious to Emma that the scroll was gone.

She felt the tears well up in her eyes. She couldn't believe how stupid she'd been. She had actually thought that Sebastian had cared for her, that he was different. She'd given all of herself to him and once again she'd been duped.

Emma thought of the tender way he'd kissed her and the gentle perusal of her body. For her that had all been so real; she thought she'd fallen in love with him last night. But for him it must have all been a ruse, something to ensure he had long enough to escape with her precious scroll.

Emma felt sick at the thought of being used in that way. She'd thought she knew Sebastian. He was kind and true. He wasn't the kind of man who tricked a woman into bed for his own gains. Or so she'd thought. She wondered if any of it had been real for him, or whether it had been an act from the very start, the performance of a lifetime.

The tears began to roll down her cheeks in earnest now. What was so wrong with her that men saw her fit only for deception and lies? And why couldn't she gauge a man's true character? Why was she always deceived by them?

She thought back to their time together over the last few weeks. They'd laughed and joked and they'd shared confidences. She had thought Sebastian to be one of the most open and honest men she'd ever met.

Stuffing her possessions back into the bag, Emma wondered what she was to do now. Sebastian had left her all on her own in the desert. She still had all the food and water...

Emma stopped still. Why hadn't he taken any of the food or water? Surely if he planned on continuing to the tomb alone and beating her to the discovery the only sensible thing to do would be to take at least half of the provisions. It didn't make sense otherwise. Even a few hours in the desert without water was enough to kill a man.

With these thoughts still circling in her head Emma quickly packed up the camp and transferred all the belongings to Wadjet. She had plenty of food and water, so her decision now was whether she should continue or whether she should turn back.

The sensible part of her knew she should turn back. If she headed due east at some point she would hit the Nile. Then it would be only a matter of hours heading either north or south until she found a settlement. But she didn't really want to go back. She wanted to confront Sebastian, to look into his eyes and make him confess how he'd deceived her.

After Freddie had so publicly disgraced her Emma had hidden in her father's house for many months, not wanting to see anyone at all, least of all Freddie. She had thought burying her head in the sand was the best way to get over what had happened to her. Now, years later, with the emotional scars still so painful, Emma knew that had been the wrong decision. If she'd been brave and had the courage to confront Freddie, make him explain to her why he'd treated her quite so badly, she might have got some closure on the event much earlier. It wouldn't have helped her reputation but it might have helped her sanity.

So this time she wasn't going to run back to Cairo and hide from Sebastian. She hadn't done anything wrong. She wanted him to face her, make him realise how much damage he'd caused.

Her heart lurched at the thought of confronting him, but she knew this time she had to stay strong. It didn't matter that just a few hours ago she'd thought she was in love with him, didn't matter that when she pictured his face and his tanned body she felt a stab of desire deep inside. He'd taken what he'd wanted from her, stolen her precious scroll and left her in the middle of the desert.

Part of her brain screamed in protest, crying that Sebastian wouldn't do that. She knew Sebastian; he would never leave a woman alone in the desert. But you couldn't argue with the evidence. Here she was all alone and Sebastian was nowhere to be seen.

Deftly Emma untied Wadjet from the dead tree and struggled to mount. The horse stood there patiently as Emma unsuccessfully tried to launch herself onto her back. After a couple of attempts Emma led Wadjet a few steps forward to where she could use a fallen tree branch to boost herself up.

Once up on the horse Emma took a few minutes to orientate herself. She knew they had been heading south-west the day before, and the plan had been to continue in that direction. Aligning herself with the sun, Emma nudged the horse forward and started her pursuit of Sebastian.

As they exited the little dried-up oasis Emma thought she saw a flash of white from the corner of her eye. It almost looked like a piece of paper. She nearly turned back to investigate, but thoughts of the gap between her and Sebastian widening stopped her from pulling on Wadjet's reins and instead she put the paper out of her mind.

Thoughts of the confrontation ahead kept Emma occupied whilst she rode. She pictured galloping up alongside Sebastian. He would look at her in shock, then fall to his knees and beg forgiveness. He would admit what a scoundrel he was and hand her back her scroll.

Even these fantasies seemed rather far-fetched to Emma. She kept returning to why he would have taken the scroll in the first place. If they found Telarti's tomb he would be credited with half the discovery alongside her. Maybe she had judged him completely wrong and he didn't care about preserving Egypt's history at all. Maybe instead he just wanted the riches inside.

It was possible, Emma supposed, but she'd seen how reverently he'd treated the scroll itself, being very gentle, as if he were touching a piece of the past.

She shook her head. It was no use trying to guess why Sebastian had done what he'd done. The fact was he'd left her in the middle of the desert and her scroll was missing. Anyone would be hard-pressed not to draw a damning conclusion from those facts.

Emma knew what she was most furious about was that she'd let herself be taken in again. After Freddie she had sworn to herself she would be wiser, more aware of the ways of the world. She had viewed men with suspicion and never until now allowed anyone to get close. But one smile from a handsome, charming man and all her resolve and common sense had deserted her. Emma knew this situation could have been avoided if only she'd hardened her heart as she'd promised herself she would so many years ago.

Chapter Twenty-Two

⚭⚭⚭

That morning Seb had awoken with a start. It was still dark, the sun wasn't even threatening to rise above the horizon for some time yet, and the fire had died down to nothing whilst they had been sleeping. Seb had wondered what had startled him awake and listened carefully for any clues the sounds of the night could give him.

For three minutes there had been nothing, not a snap of a twig or a cry of a bird. Just as Seb had been about to lie back down a soft noise had come to his ear. It had been the snorting of a horse still some way away.

He had frozen completely and listened. He hadn't been able to hear the plod of hooves or the scrape of stones as they were dislodged, which meant whoever was approaching had been still a little way off. There was a possibility that it had been just a random traveller, a

Bedouin trekking across the desert back to his people, but Seb knew that was unlikely.

Now, four hours later, Seb wished he'd quietly woken Emma and explained his concerns to her. Instead he'd thought he'd be the hero of the day and get rid of their pursuers without Emma even realising he'd gone.

Seb had dressed quickly and gathered up a few necessities. He'd only planned on being away from their little camp for about an hour, so he'd only taken a small amount of water to sustain him. Then he'd rummaged through Emma's bag until his fingers had closed around the scroll. For a second Seb had just revelled in the feel of the old papyrus, but, knowing time was of the essence, he had slipped the scroll into a sock and placed it back in the bag, now nicely hidden just in case his plan went wrong.

The last thing he'd done before leaving the camp was scribble a quick note to Emma just in case she woke up before he returned. He hadn't wanted her to wake up and find him gone with no explanation. He'd left it close to where she was sleeping, so it would be the first thing she saw when she woke up and realised he had gone.

Gently he'd leaned over and kissed her on the cheek, then he'd mounted his horse and left the camp. When he'd been a few minutes away he'd stopped and listened. Sure enough their pursuers had been even closer. He'd made sure his horse made plenty of noise to draw them away from the camp and set off into the darkness.

That had been four hours ago. Now Seb was parched and sweating in the early morning sun. He'd drunk his last drop of water at least an hour ago and already he felt as though his tongue had swelled to fill his mouth. His body was screaming out for water and he knew if he didn't find a way to head back to their camp soon he would collapse.

Seb wished now he'd thought of a different plan. One that involved having Emma by his side and plenty of water in his water skin. He cursed himself again, knowing that it was his need to always be in control that drove him to do things like this. He hoped desperately Emma had found the note he'd left her and had followed his instructions to wait for him at the old oasis, stringing up a blanket to form some shade to rest in. She should be comfortable enough, but he had no doubt she would be annoyed with him when he returned. He'd never planned on being away this long.

He pictured her soft body in his arms and

grinned. He was sure he could persuade her to let him make it up to her if she was angry.

Seb heard the distant ring of voices and quickly looked over his shoulder. For the last hour he'd heard further evidence of his pursuers and he knew they were getting closer. He'd tried to lead them away from Emma and her precious scroll, and his plan had been to loop back to camp before they realised, but he hadn't counted on how fast they were. He knew if he looped back now they would be close enough to follow.

Frowning, he tried to spur his horse on, but the animal was also suffering from the lack of water.

Every minute the voices grew louder and then suddenly there was a shout. Seb knew they must have caught sight of him, but there was nowhere to run and most certainly nowhere to hide. At least when they caught up with him maybe they would have some water.

He turned to face the four men approaching him, watching as their black robes billowed out as their horses trotted towards him. They did not smile or exchange words of victory; instead all four seemed to remain completely serious.

Seb dismounted as they approached, thinking it would be sensible to seem as unthreatening as possible. They rode up and surrounded him, throwing a cloud of dust into the air. Seb coughed, the dust tickling his already dry throat, and the spasms made him bend double.

'Where is the woman?' one of the men asked in flawless English.

'Water,' Seb gasped as he straightened up.

No one moved for a few seconds. Then the man who had spoken—Seb took him to be the leader of the little group—gave a quick, curt nod. Another one of the bandits took out a water skin and threw it at Seb.

He drank slowly, unhurriedly, knowing if he put too much water in his shrivelled stomach it would just make him sick. Instead he savoured the warm liquid in his mouth before swallowing slowly.

When he had had his fill he passed the water skin back to the bandit.

'Now, where is the woman?' the leader asked again.

Seb shrugged. 'Halfway back to Luxor by now,' he said nonchalantly.

The bandits frowned.

'She was with you until last night.'

Seb nodded, not giving away any more than he had to.

'Why would she decide to go back to Luxor this morning? Alone and unprotected.'

'Stupid woman made her decision,' he said. 'I wasn't going to try and stop her.'

The leader smiled, revealing a mouthful of yellowed teeth.

'Please don't lie to me, Mr Oakfield. You have come this far in her company, why would you part ways now?'

Seb sighed dramatically and looked up at the bandit.

'We were following some sort of map. A day ago she lost it. She said there was no point continuing without the map to guide her.'

'And you disagreed?'

'By then I'd say anything to get away from her. We rowed. She rode off. I thought I'd continue.'

'Without the map to guide you?'

'I knew what general direction we were headed. It couldn't harm to take a look.'

The bandit looked at him long and hard.

'I don't believe a word you are saying, Mr Oakfield. Firstly we know your reputation. You would not leave a woman to fend for herself in the desert.'

Seb opened his mouth to protest but the bandit silenced him by holding up another finger.

'Secondly, you expect us to believe a man who has made hundreds of trips into the desert would continue his latest expedition without even a day's supply of water.'

They had him there. Seb knew no man who had ever been into the desert would do so again without at least double the amount of water he needed for his trip.

'No, I think Miss Knight is camped somewhere nearby, patiently awaiting your return. And you thought to draw us away from her and her map, not realising quite how close we were.'

Well, they were almost right, Seb thought, although he doubted Emma was patiently awaiting his return. He resisted the urge to take out his pocket watch and check the time. In his note he'd told Emma not to wait for him past midday, urging her instead to head back towards Luxor. He hoped now she had done so and wasn't delaying her departure to give him extra time to return to her.

'Why don't you make this easy on yourself, Mr Oakfield? Take us to where Miss Knight is waiting and I give you my word you shall both be safe.'

Seb looked up at the bandit and knew he couldn't trust the man. He had no doubt that as soon as he got his hands on the scroll both he and Emma would become an inconvenience. An inconvenience that could quite easily be dealt with and a whole desert to leave the bodies in.

'She's turned back to Luxor,' Seb repeated.

'Tell me about this map,' the bandit said, changing his line of questioning.

'I never saw it properly. Miss Knight was very secretive.'

'You must have had a look when she was asleep?'

Seb shrugged. 'It was dark. I had a look but the detail wasn't clear.'

'Tell me what you did see.'

'There was a seal of sorts in the corner, then a series of landmarks before a big cross.'

The bandit's eyes lit up and Seb wondered why this man was so eager to get his hands on the scroll and find the tomb. He couldn't work out if he was a grave robber or a man wanting to protect his heritage at any cost.

'I will get my hands on that scroll, Mr Oakfield. What I do with you and your companion afterwards very much depends on how helpful you are now.'

Seb met the man's stare steadily and didn't look away. After half a minute the bandit snorted and looked at his henchmen.

'Tie Mr Oakfield's hands in front of him and secure him to a horse. We shall rest before we begin our search.'

Seb hid a smile. Every moment they delayed gave Emma longer to get away, to head back to Luxor and to the safety of the crowds. He didn't resist as one of the bandits tied his hands securely in front of him and tied the other end of the rope to the reins of his horse. Seb realised he was going to be made to stumble behind them, pulled along if he lost his footing, his skin shredded by the sand.

Quickly he flexed his knees to make sure he was limbered up and ready for this bit of exercise. The last thing he wanted was to fall on his face and lose half his skin.

Thankfully they moved off at quite a slow pace and Seb found it easy enough to follow behind. Only when they started their descent into a dried-up river bed did he have to increase his pace, ever aware of the loose sand and rocks beneath his feet. But he was nimble and reached the bottom without missing a step. A little farther along the river bed they reached a large rock, twice the height of any man. The bandit leader indicated they would stop here in the shade.

Seb waited as the man riding the horse he was tied to dismounted. Then he watched as the same man expertly untied his hands from in front of him and securely bound them behind him again. He flexed his wrists and found there was little movement and every small adjustment in position meant the ropes chafed his skin. If he tried to wriggle too much his wrists would be red raw.

Reluctantly Seb sat down in the shade. He glanced up at the sky and noted the position of the sun. If Emma hadn't already set off for Luxor earlier, hopefully she would have done by now. The sun was high above him and Seb knew it must be about midday. Hopefully she would reach the city within a day or two and find shelter there.

Chapter Twenty-Three

Emma was feeling rather pleased with herself. Living her sheltered life in England, she had never been taught to track animals through the woods, as many boys were expected to do. Now, however, she was feeling an expert.

After about an hour of riding Emma had begun to notice a disturbance in the dust. At first she had wondered what on earth it could be, then it had hit her; she was following in some-one else's trail.

Now Emma knew this wasn't necessarily Sebastian's trail, but in her mind it was quite likely. After all, how many people would be riding through the middle of the desert in this exact spot? It was easy to follow; the dusty trail made for an easy path to pursue Sebastian on.

As she rode she contemplated how she would confront Sebastian. She wondered whether she should be cold and efficient, riding up to him and demanding her scroll back with no emotion on her face. She wouldn't mention their night together, as if it had meant nothing to her.

Although Emma would love to do that, she knew it would likely be impossible. She knew as soon as she saw Sebastian she would be overcome with emotion. Hurt and betrayal would rise up inside her and she would need to know why he had done it. Not why he had stolen her scroll—that was pretty obvious—but why he had seduced her and then so cruelly left her.

She also wanted to know whether anything he'd told her the night before had been the truth. He had seemed to pour his heart out to her, confiding in her the horrors of his childhood, but now Emma wondered if it was a practised ploy to get women to take that final step and go to bed with him.

A flash of memory hit her, Sebastian's hands gently roaming over her body, a wondrous smile on his face, and Emma had to struggle to suppress it. She didn't want to think of their night together. She didn't want to dwell on the fact that once again she'd been taken in by a man who just wanted to use her.

The anger and fury swelled up inside her

again and Emma spurred Wadjet forward. She was going to catch up with Sebastian soon and when she did she would make him look her in the eye and admit everything he'd done. It probably wouldn't make her feel any better, but at least she would know this time she'd had the courage to face the man who'd betrayed her.

She'd been riding for a couple of hours when the trail seemed to lead her down into a dried-up river bed. Emma carefully let Wadjet pick a path through the loose stones and dust and then gently pulled on the reins to bring the horse to a stop. The ground down here was made up of loose stones and the trail Emma had been following seemed to disappear. She studied both directions, wondering which way to go, knowing she had to be careful not to lose her bearings; in the desert that could be deadly.

Emma felt a cloud of despair fall over her. All the time she had been following in Sebastian's trail she had felt a sense of purpose that had overshadowed her underlying feelings of betrayal. Now, with no way to know which direction Sebastian had chosen, she felt the tears start to well up in her eyes.

Silently she berated herself. She'd brought this on herself. Tears wouldn't help her find Sebastian and get her scroll back and they wouldn't change the past.

Decisively she urged Wadjet round to the left. The horse was slow to respond, instead turning her head back to the right, ears pricked up as if listening to something.

Emma listened, too. Then she broke out into a smile. She could hear something: just the quiet hum of voices, too far to make out what they were saying, but voices all the same.

Conscious that Sebastian might anticipate her following him, Emma dismounted and slowly led Wadjet towards the voices, taking each step slowly. Within five minutes the distant hum had become much more distinctive and Emma could catch a few words.

'Would you care for some water, Mr Oakfield?'

Emma grimaced. No doubt Sebastian had met up with some travelling companions, people who would help him excavate the tomb once they'd followed the map on her scroll.

Fury building up inside her, Emma marched round the corner of the river bed and then froze.

Her mouth hung open in surprise and the words of recrimination froze on her tongue.

Squatting on the floor of the river bed were

four men dressed in all-black robes. Sebastian was also nearby, but, far from being served by these men, he was dishevelled and tied up; he was their prisoner.

Emma tried to take a step back round the corner, but that was when one of the men saw her. He jumped to his feet, followed closely by his three companions, and reached her in a couple of strides. Emma gasped as he drew a curved sword and held it out towards her, whilst grabbing her arm with his free hand.

Her eyes met Sebastian's and she saw a flash of anger followed by a deep look of concern. He strained against the ropes that bound him and struggled to his feet, only to be pushed down again by another of the men.

'Miss Knight, I presume,' one of the bandits said in perfect English.

There was no point denying it. What other Englishwoman would be foolish enough to be wandering around the desert alone?

'Not quite the route to Luxor I would have chosen.'

'Take your hands off her,' Sebastian said, his voice low and dangerous.

'I think we shall keep hold of Miss Knight for now, but do not fear. We mean her no harm.'

The bandit walked closer to Emma and she tried not to cower away. He was terrifying. Half his face was covered in a jet-black beard and his eyes were intense and piercing. Emma frowned, she'd looked into those eyes before. Then it hit her: this man had been the intruder in her room when she had been staying with the Fitzgeralds.

'You have something I want, Miss Knight. Give it to me and you shall not be harmed.'

'What about Mr Oakfield?' Emma asked, her voice shaking. She might not know what to think about Sebastian's abandonment of her now, but whatever had happened, she didn't want him to die at the end of this bandit's sword.

'Yes, yes, yes. Mr Oakfield will be safe, too.'

'What do you want?' she asked, trying to exude confidence she did not have.

'Your scroll.'

Emma swallowed. 'I'm sorry, but I seem to have misplaced it. Otherwise I would gladly give it to you.'

The bandit stepped closer to her so their faces were only a few inches apart. She could feel his breath on her cheeks and had to resist the urge to take a step back.

'I'm in no mood for games, Miss Knight. Tell

me where the scroll is or I will have to become a lot more unpleasant.'

Emma knew she probably wouldn't survive if the bandit didn't get what he wanted, but equally she couldn't give him something she didn't have.

She stole a glance at Sebastian, who was now being held down by two of the bandits. He continued to struggle and as she watched he received a punch to the stomach for his efforts.

'I don't have the scroll,' Emma said, marvelling that the words even came out of her mouth, she was so nervous.

'Cut off an ear,' the bandit said, motioning towards Sebastian.

'No,' Emma gasped. 'Please, I don't have the scroll. When I woke up this morning it had disappeared along with Mr Oakfield.'

The bandit turned back to Sebastian and took a step towards him.

'So you lied earlier. You do have the scroll.'

Sebastian shook his head. 'No,' he gasped, his breathing still heavy from the punch in the stomach.

The bandit reached out for Emma and pulled her towards him. She tried to wriggle free from his grip as he held her against his chest but his arms were too strong and he held her easily.

'I think you know where the scroll is, Mr Oakfield,' the bandit said, running the curved edge of the blade across Emma's cheek.

She shuddered and felt her legs give way beneath her. The bandit held her upright and continued to caress her cheek with the blade.

'It would be such a shame to mar Miss Knight's beautiful white skin, but I am not prepared to listen to your lies any longer. Tell me where the scroll is or I'll start with her nose.'

Sebastian seemed to sag against the two men holding him.

'In the bag,' he said, motioning behind Emma to where Wadjet stood patiently.

All four bandits and Emma turned to look at the horse. One of the men stepped towards the beast and caught hold of her reins. Quickly he unstrapped the bag Sebastian had indicated and turned it upside down.

Emma frowned. She knew the scroll wasn't in the bag because she'd checked it this morning and she wondered what Sebastian was doing. He was certainly playing a dangerous game, and it was her life that he was putting in danger

The bandit started rummaging through the contents that were now spread across the ground. Emma peered curiously at the assortment of clothes and belongings. There was definitely no scroll.

'I don't see the scroll, Mr Oakfield,' the bandit said as he tightened his grip on Emma again.

'In one of the socks,' Sebastian said with a sigh.

Emma watched as each sock was shaken out in turn, until on the third attempt a very familiar rolled-up scroll fell out onto the desert floor.

'But…' Emma said, her eyes wide with incredulity.

'You thought I'd stolen it from you?' Sebastian asked softly.

Emma couldn't bring her eyes up to meet his.

'Tie her up whilst we decide what to do with them,' the bandit said, pushing Emma towards one of his men. His eyes were fixed on the scroll and he seemed to have lost interest in his prisoners now the prize was within his grasp.

As Emma was pushed down beside Sebastian she felt his eyes boring into her, but still she couldn't bring herself to look at him. She knew she'd made a terrible mistake and now she and Sebastian were paying for it.

Chapter Twenty-Four

Seb couldn't bring himself to look at Emma. He felt angry, angrier than he'd ever felt before. Not at her, but at the danger he'd placed her in. If he was any kind of gentleman he would have refused to bring her on this foolhardy trip, he would have insisted she stay safe in Cairo, attending dinners and dances and visiting the new Museum of Antiquities. Instead here she was, trussed up and the prisoner of some very dangerous men.

Seb didn't know what the bandits were planning on doing with them, but he doubted it would be anything good. If they left them alive both Seb and Emma would be able to identify them, and that was dangerous. It would be much easier to kill them out here in the desert, bury the bodies and have the world assume they'd got lost in a sandstorm and died of dehydration or exposure.

'Sebastian,' Emma whispered.

He turned to face her and saw the tears running down her cheeks.

'It'll all work out,' he said gruffly.

'I'm so sorry.'

He looked at her and realised she was crying because she thought he was angry with her.

He had to admit he did feel a bit hurt she'd assumed that he'd taken off with her scroll, that he'd made love to her then abandoned her in the cold light of day.

Seb knew Emma had an issue with trust—she had good reason to, she'd been hurt before and just assumed it would happen again—but he had hoped she would have started to trust him over the last few weeks. He had hoped she would not assume the worst.

'You were gone and I couldn't find the scroll and I didn't know what to think.'

'So you assumed I'd stolen it and left you alone in the middle of the desert?' Seb regretted the words as soon as they were out of his mouth. He didn't want to make Emma feel any worse than she already did. What he really wanted was to put his arms around her and tell her that everything would turn out well. But he couldn't do that. Unfortunately his hands were tied securely and even worse he didn't know they were going to be all right.

'I'm sorry,' Emma whispered again.

'Don't apologise,' Seb said. 'I should never have left you alone.'

He cursed his decision for the hundredth time. It was pure pride that had made him leave Emma sleeping in the camp whilst he tried to lure their pursuers away. At the time he had told himself that he hadn't wanted to worry her, but the truth was much less noble. He had wanted to be the big hero, Emma's protector, to draw away the bandits and be back triumphant before Emma was even awake. Look where that pride had got them now.

'It was stupid and reckless and if anything happens to you I'll never forgive myself.'

'I'm sorry. I should have…' Emma started again.

Seb shuffled a little closer to her, keeping one eye on the bandits who were engrossed in studying the scroll.

'Don't apologise,' he repeated. 'This whole thing is my fault.'

'Why didn't you tell me you were leaving?'

Seb smiled ruefully. 'I thought I'd be the hero and lead our pursuers away whilst you were sleeping and be back before you awoke.'

'So you were going to come back?' Emma asked, her voice small.

Seb saw all the years of hurt and rejection on her face. Freddie had destroyed much of her confidence and now he'd nearly ruined the remaining shreds. He hoped the damage wasn't irreversible.

'For the last few hours I've thought of nothing but you. I wanted to be back beside you with all my heart. Did you not see my note?'

Emma looked at him searchingly and Seb felt as if she were looking into his soul. Finally she shook her head.

'I left it right in front of you.'

'There was no note, Sebastian.'

Seb shook his head as he realised the note must have become dislodged and blown away in the gentle desert breeze.

'I promise you I was going to come back.'

Emma looked him directly in the eye then nodded. She believed him.

'So what went wrong?' she asked.

'They were much closer than I realised. I

thought I'd be able to set a false trail for them, then double back to our camp before it got light.'

'How did you know they were following us?' Emma asked, as if this had just occurred to her.

'Someone's been following us since we left Cairo. When the boys were with us it was easier to keep watch. Since they left for Luxor it's been more difficult.'

'Why didn't you tell me?'

'I didn't want to worry you.' And he'd had this stupid notion of being her protector.

'You see the man holding the scroll? Their leader?' Emma asked. 'He ransacked my room at the Fitzgeralds' whilst I was staying there.'

Seb felt his mouth open with surprise.

'You knew you could be in danger?'

Emma shrugged. 'I never thought anyone would go to this length to get their hands on the scroll.'

Seb shifted slightly and watched the four men squatting on the ground. They were talking animatedly and gesturing wildly. All four men seemed very excited by what they saw.

'What are we going to do?' Emma asked.

Seb didn't answer for a minute or two.

'We need to escape,' he said eventually.

'With the scroll,' Emma prompted.

He frowned at her. 'The most important thing is that you get away safely. I do not give a damn about that scroll. I'd trade one hundred scrolls for your safety.'

He saw her start to smile and wanted to reach out and shake her.

'I'm serious, Emma. You must promise me if an opportunity arises you'll run. Without the scroll and without me if needs be.'

He saw the colour drain from her cheeks.

'Not without you,' she said.

'I'm not planning on getting killed, but you are my priority here. If there is a chance you can escape without me then you have to take it.'

She shook her head stubbornly. 'I'm not leaving you behind.'

'Please, Emma.' Seb could hear the desperation in his voice.

She shook her head again. 'We will escape and we will escape together.'

Seb was about to continue the argument when the leader of the bandits stood and started to walk towards them.

'Quiet,' he barked.

Both Seb and Emma closed their mouths firmly, but Seb sidled even closer to Emma's side. He wasn't sure what he could do tied up quite so tightly, but if this criminal even looked at Emma in the wrong way he would attack him with everything he had.

'The scroll is very beautiful,' the bandit said, directing his words at Emma. 'Just as I had been led to believe.'

Seb saw Emma frown beside him but thankfully she bit her tongue and didn't utter a word.

'It is good to have such a valuable treasure back in our family.'

'What?' Emma asked sharply.

'How do you think your father came into possession of this piece of our heritage?' The bandit was smiling now, obviously trying to goad Emma.

Seb sensed her stiffen beside him and wished he could reach out a hand to try and calm her down.

'I don't know what you are suggesting but my father was an honourable man.'

The bandit shook his head slowly, clearly enjoying taunting Emma.

'An honourable man wouldn't have taken such a valuable artefact from our country.'

'If he was the rightful owner he could do whatever he liked with it. Your family shouldn't have been so careless as to lose it in the first place.'

Seb felt the muscles in his legs tense as his body got ready to attack. He could see anger lurking just behind the bandit's smile. A few more inflammatory words from Emma and who knew what he would do?

'My grandfather lost the scroll in a wager,' the bandit spat. 'An unfair wager that your father should never have agreed to.'

'You can't blame my father for your grandfather's unwise betting actions.' Emma was almost laughing, seemingly unaware of the danger she was putting herself in.

'An honourable man would have refused the wager if he already knew the outcome.'

The bandit crouched down so he was level with Emma.

'Why don't we have a little wager now?' he asked, his eyes glinting maliciously.

Seb wished he could do something to intervene. He hated feeling so helpless. Every fibre in his body wanted to launch itself at the bandit and batter him into the ground, but he knew with his hands tied as they were he had no chance of beating four able-bodied men. He might succeed in knocking one or two to the ground, but he knew before he could do any more he'd have a sword through his gut and then Emma would be truly alone.

'I wager that you won't escape this desert alive.'

Seb watched as all the blood drained from Emma's face. He wondered if she would swoon, but he saw her rally herself, set her shoulders and tilt her chin ever so slightly upwards.

'And if you win?' she asked.

The bandit laughed, as did his three companions. Seb started to feel sick to his stomach.

'If you can escape by nightfall tomorrow night then you win your life. If you don't...' he left the sentence trailing for a few seconds '...then you'll be begging me to kill you when the time comes.'

Seb felt Emma lean against him and he knew she realised the implications of the bandit's words.

'So if we escape by tomorrow night you'll let us live, you won't pursue us?' Emma asked.

Seb could have kissed her. She was so brave and strong, much braver and stronger than she gave herself credit for.

He saw the momentary frown cross the

bandit's face. He'd obviously wanted to scare her more.

The bandit nodded curtly.

'Deal,' she said.

After a few seconds the bandit snorted.

'This is not a wager I will let you win, Miss Knight.'

Chapter Twenty-Five

Emma felt her whole body start to shake. She watched the bandit walk away and knew if he turned back he would see how terrified she was. All the time he'd been looking at her Emma had managed to keep herself under control, but now she felt as though she wanted to cry and scream at the same time.

Emma felt Sebastian's body press against hers. She felt the warmth and the strength emanating from him and she felt just a tiny bit more in control.

'You were very brave,' he said, soothing. 'You just close your eyes and relax for a few seconds.'

Emma closed her eyes and tried to deepen her breathing, but the bandit's face seemed to be seared onto the insides of her eyelids, gloating at her discomfort. Quickly Emma opened her eyes again and instead looked at Sebastian.

'I will never let that man do anything to you,' Sebastian said.

Emma looked deep into his eyes and she knew she believed him. Right now they might be tied up and completely at the bandit's mercy, but she believed Sebastian would do anything to protect her. That was just the kind of man he was.

'I will not let him touch you,' he said, not breaking eye contact with her.

Emma felt some of the panic begin to subside.

'You will be safe.'

Even though right now it seemed impossible to imagine, Emma believed him. She didn't know how he planned to escape, defeat four heavily armed bandits and find their way out of the desert, but if anyone could do it, Sebastian would.

'I don't know why he hates me so much,' Emma said quietly, her voice shaking a little.

'It doesn't matter,' Sebastian said. 'In a few days this will all just be a distant memory.'

Emma nodded. 'So how will we escape?'

Before Sebastian could answer the bandits were on their feet and Emma felt her body stiffen once again. She wondered whether they would stick to the wager and leave her alone until tomorrow night, and a shiver of fear spread through her body.

'On your feet,' the chief bandit ordered.

Emma struggled to stand with her hands tied, but managed to stumble to her feet.

'I advise you keep up,' the bandit said.

Emma's eyes widened with disbelief as the end of the rope securing her hands was tied to one of the bandit's horses. She eyed Wadjet and wondered why she couldn't ride. It took a few more minutes to secure Sebastian; his hands had been tied behind his back so one of the bandits had to untie him and secure his hands in front of him before tying his rope to the horse.

'We will not stop for anything,' the bandit warned as they set off at a slow walk.

Emma felt the muscles in her legs protest as they started to walk. She had been sitting in a crunched position for a while and her muscles wanted stretching, but there was no time for that. She knew after a few minutes of walking she would warm up. Her injured ankle also screamed in protest the first few steps they took, but thankfully after a little while the pain dulled to a manageable ache.

Sebastian was a few yards ahead of her and she could see he kept glancing over his shoulder to check she was still on her feet. As she walked she studied his back and wondered at his reaction to her accusing him of stealing her scroll.

He'd protested that he wasn't angry with her, and she believed him, but she was sure she'd hurt him with her lack of trust. Emma knew now he had only been trying to protect her, and she'd assumed the worst. Deep down she'd known Sebastian was a kind and good man, but still she hadn't been able to trust that he would come back to her.

She wondered if she'd ruined any hope of a future they had together. The previous night they hadn't spoken about what their intimacy had meant, but Emma knew Sebastian wasn't the sort of man to make love to a woman of good birth and just walk away. That had been why they'd resisted each other for so long in the first place. But now, after Emma had shown she didn't trust him, Sebastian would be perfectly within his rights to leave her. Why should he go against everything he believed in for a woman who couldn't even have faith he hadn't stolen from her?

She felt a lump form in her throat and tried to push it away. Now wasn't the time to start crying; she had to focus on surviving the next twenty-four hours.

Images of what their life could have been like started to form in Emma's mind. She saw them strolling hand in hand through the streets of Cairo, smiling at each other over dinner and maybe even doting on a little baby of their own.

Emma physically shook her head to banish the images. She had no doubt their lives could have been that happy, if only she had trusted Sebastian. Now she had destroyed any hope of that future and there was no point dwelling on it. For years she had been quite content knowing she would grow old with only herself for company, but that had been before Sebastian, before she had realised what her life could have been like. Now she would have to get used to the idea of living without the man she loved.

Emma stumbled and gasped. She saw Sebastian glance round and she gave him a shaky smile to assure him she was all right. In truth she hadn't tripped on a rock or lost her footing on some loose gravel, but she had realised the truth behind her thoughts— she loved Sebastian.

The words seemed to keep spinning around in her head and Emma felt as though she wanted to catch hold of them and examine them. Could she really love Sebastian? She'd only known him for a couple of weeks. And only a few hours ago she was ready to believe he had stolen from her.

Emma shook her head; that wasn't a reason not to love Sebastian. That was a reason she had to work on her own issues. She knew she lacked trust. If she couldn't trust a man like Sebastian, someone who had sacrificed so much for her already, surely she had no hope of sharing her life with another?

She studied Sebastian's back and wondered whether she would feel the same way about him had they met in different circumstances. If they'd met at a ball in London would her heart pound in the same way every time he was near? Emma had to admit it would. It wasn't the exotic location or the excitement of their adventures together that made her heart swell with love every time he got close: it was purely Sebastian, the man. From the very first moment she'd laid eyes on him she'd felt the quickening of her pulse, and that initial attraction had grown into something much, much more over the last few weeks.

Sebastian suddenly glanced back towards her and caught her staring. Emma smiled sheepishly. She saw him check they weren't being observed then he winked at her. With a frown spreading across her face Emma wondered what he was up to. Nothing happened for a few minutes and she started to question whether her overheated mind had imagined the wink. Then, without any further warning, Sebastian stumbled and fell to the floor. Emma heard the gasp leave her lips and she tried to run forward to help him up. The bandits were already pulling on his rope, but to Emma's dismay she could see they weren't slowing down at all. She started to imagine Sebastian being dragged through the desert on his knees, his skin ripped to shreds by the rocky desert floor.

Before she could reach his side Sebastian had staggered back to his feet. His clothes were covered with dust and she could see one trouser leg was ripped at the knee. She wondered if he had injured himself and thought about begging the bandits to stop. She was just about to open her mouth when Sebastian turned back to her and winked again.

Emma froze, her mouth hanging open. She wondered what he was playing at. Surely his trip hadn't been engineered—what would have been the point in injuring himself?

Sebastian quickly turned to face forward again and Emma continued to stare at him. He gave no further indication of what he was planning and Emma wished they were closer so she could ask him.

After another twenty minutes of trudging through the desert Emma was convinced she must have imagined the winks. Sebastian was now acting like the model prisoner, walking along behind the bandit's horse without even the slightest protest. Emma had no doubt Sebastian was working on a way to save her, but she couldn't see how falling to his knees in the desert could possibly be part of that.

For the last couple of hours Emma had been desperately trying not to think about what was to become of them. She knew the bandits wouldn't let them go. It would be stupid to set free two prisoners who could identify them easily and had the ears of some of the most influential men in Egypt within their circles. Emma knew if they didn't somehow escape they'd be left as carrion for the birds.

She wondered bleakly who would miss her. Ahmed would certainly shed a tear, but she'd been forced to step back from many of her old friends after the Freddie scandal and the truth was she didn't have many people who would mourn her life.

Emma tried to banish the maudlin thoughts. Sebastian had said he would get her out of the desert alive and she believed him. It might seem an impossible feat now, but Sebastian was a man of his word, and she trusted him.

She shook her head in wonder at the truth of the matter. She did trust him. Despite her convictions just a few hours before, she trusted Sebastian. For Emma this was rather a big realisation. For years, since Freddie had humiliated her in quite such a public fashion, Emma hadn't really trusted anyone but her father and Ahmed, but now there was also Sebastian.

He might be unconventional but he was most certainly trustworthy, and Emma knew if anyone could get them out of this situation then Sebastian, with his quick mind and his unwavering sense of right and wrong, was the man who could.

She couldn't help but giggle. It had taken being captured by bandits for Emma to realise she trusted Sebastian. And more than that—that she loved him. She only hoped they both survived this ordeal so she could tell him her feelings and declare her love.

Chapter Twenty-Six

Seb started to whistle. The action got him a clip around the ear from one of the bandits, but it was worth it. He was feeling optimistic.

He'd been in many a scrape over the years and he was a little ashamed to admit this wasn't even the most dangerous situation he'd got himself into, but it was the worst. It was the worst because this time it wasn't just his life on the line, but Emma's, too. Seb quite cheerfully risked life and limb on almost a monthly basis, but never had he been responsible for someone else's well-being.

He glanced back at Emma again. She was looking at him strangely, studying him quite intently, probably watching for a further signal. When Seb had winked earlier he'd hoped she would understand the meaning. He'd just wanted to tell her he had a plan and everything would work out all right.

Surreptitiously Seb began working on his escape whilst making sure not to change his facial expression. The bandits might only look at him occasionally, but one glance at the wrong moment and their only chance to survive would be gone.

He kept checking the position of the sun in the sky and was relieved to see they still had a couple of hours until sunset. That gave him a couple of hours before they made camp and he'd have to make his move. Seb hoped Emma survived the trek through the desert until then. The bandits hadn't offered them any water in the few hours they'd been walking, and even though the pace was slow the heat was draining. He shook his head. Emma would be fine—she was a resilient woman, more resilient than he'd given her credit for. She had survived without a single grumble for nearly two weeks in the desert with him, and when he'd disappeared she'd tracked him down. Not many women were capable of that.

An hour later the bandits slowed so they were lined up beside each other. Seb focussed on what they were saying in rapid Arabic and realised to his dismay they were thinking about stopping for the night. He needed just one more hour, maybe even forty-five minutes, but if they stopped now he wouldn't be ready for his escape plan.

Thankfully one of the bandits shook his head and gestured to a point on the horizon, somewhere he felt would make a better camp, so slowly they started to move again. For a few steps Seb was beside Emma.

'Are you well?' he asked quietly.

She nodded, her eyes wide. Seb could see her lips were dry and on the point of cracking and he cursed the bandits for not giving her even a sip of water.

Before he could say any more Seb felt his rope being tugged forward at quite a pace and he had to run to keep up.

'You know our rules on talking, Mr Oakfield,' the chief bandit said.

Seb didn't bother to reply.

'I think my horse needs some exercise.'

Immediately Seb tensed. He knew exactly what was going to happen; he just hoped the bandits limited their fun to him and not Emma.

After a few seconds Seb saw the bandit kick his horse forward and the rope went tight. At first they were travelling at a light trot, which Seb easily kept up with, but he knew things were only going to get worse. Beside him he saw the other bandits' horses pick up the pace and a quick glance over his shoulder confirmed his fear: Emma was now being pulled along behind. She was still on her feet, but one misstep and she would have her delicate, beautiful skin ripped from her by the desert.

The chief bandit called out in Arabic and Seb felt himself relax a little. He'd just instructed his companion not to spoil the woman, otherwise they wouldn't enjoy her as much later on. Although it was a chilling command, Seb wasn't planning on letting Emma be around later on, and knowing they wouldn't drag her through the desert now meant he could focus on staying on his own feet rather than worrying about her.

The bandit threw him a glance and smiled, then urged his horse onwards. Immediately Seb's legs started to protest and his heart began hammering in his chest. He was running now, the movement clumsy with his arms tied in front of him, and he felt his chest heave as he tried to suck in the hot desert air to sustain him. Seb focussed his eyes on the ground, knowing one trip, one misstep and he was going to be skinned alive.

Just when Seb thought he couldn't take much more he saw the bandit push the horse to go even faster. Seb knew his limits, he knew at this sprinting pace he could only keep up for a minute, at the most two, then his legs would give out and turn to jelly underneath him.

Just as the fatigue was setting in and Seb waited for the inevitable he felt the pace slow slightly. His lungs were screaming out for oxygen and his muscles felt as though he'd just climbed a mountain, but he was still on his feet.

Thankfully the bandit was slowing to a stop and Seb took the opportunity to glance around him. This must be where they were going to set up camp for the night. The soft undulations of the desert had made this spot into a high point, giving it a good view of the surrounding area. The bandits would be well set up to keep watch for anyone approaching their camp, or indeed see the path of any escapees very easily.

Seb was just getting his breath back when he heard a high-pitched scream. His heart leapt into his throat as he spun around. Emma was still a hundred feet away, the bandit pulling her along had slowed to a trot, but she'd somehow lost her footing and was now on her knees. The momentum of the horse kept pulling her forward even as the bandit urged the beast to stop and it was a good ten seconds before she was still.

Seb wanted to run to her, to scoop her into his arms and check she wasn't seriously injured, but he knew that would be disastrous. He'd spent most of the walk across the desert that afternoon chipping away at the ropes that bound his hands with a sharp stone he'd picked up when he had feigned his fall. Now he was sure he could slip out of his bonds but it would give away every advantage he had. So instead he stood, waiting for Emma to move, hoping she hadn't sustained any serious injuries.

The bandit scooped her up onto his horse, laying her across his lap, and a minute later they arrived. Seb strained to see whether Emma's eyes were open. She could have easily hit her head as she fell and he felt his whole body tense with anticipation. He couldn't lose her, he just couldn't.

As they came nearer Seb saw Emma's eyes flutter open. Immediately she grimaced and her whole body tensed. He wished he could take away the pain she must be feeling, wished it were him with the skin ripped from his legs and not her.

The bandit lowered her to the ground and dismounted, looking sheepishly at the leader. He received a cuff round the head for his carelessness, but Seb wanted to do so much more to him. He felt the rage simmer inside him, but as Emma glanced his way he managed to suppress it. He had to control himself or they would lose their one opportunity to escape and these men would make Emma suffer in unimaginable ways.

Seeing that Emma was still conscious and more or less in one piece, the chief bandit picked her up, carried her a few steps and deposited her beside Sebastian. Then, without even really looking at Seb, he tied Emma to the same horse Seb was secured to and ensured all four horses were tied together. The chief bandit turned away and quickly shouted instructions for his men to set up camp.

'Emma?' Seb whispered quietly.

He could hear her crying beside him, but her head was hanging forward and he couldn't see her face.

Slowly she lifted her chin and looked at him. Her skin was ashen underneath the dust and her tears ran in rivulets down her cheeks. She had a small scrape just above her eyebrow. Seb felt his breath catch in his throat. Even like this she was beautiful.

'Where are you hurt?'

'My…my legs,' she stuttered.

Seb looked down but all he could see in the fading light were torn trousers, some of the fabric stained with blood.

He lifted his eyes once again to her face and leaned in closer.

'I'm going to get you out of here,' he promised.

Emma looked into his eyes for a long few seconds before finally nodding.

Seb leant forward and caught her lips with his, kissing her ever so gently.

'I'm going to get you out of here then I'll never let anything bad happen to you again.'

A shout from the bandits made them spring apart and Seb watched warily as the chief bandit made his way over to them.

'I didn't have you down for a selfish man, Mr Oakfield,' he said, his voice mocking.

Seb stayed quiet, knowing if he put any of his thoughts into words it would only antagonise the bandit.

'You have a beautiful thing here—' he gestured at Emma '—but you aren't prepared to share with the rest of us.'

Seb felt his body stiffen.

'Leave Miss Knight alone,' he said, his voice hard and cold.

'I don't think you're in a position to make threats, Mr Oakfield.'

He pulled Emma to her feet and Seb watched as she bit her lip to try and hide the pain she was in.

'I can see the appeal,' the bandit said. 'I normally prefer my women less dusty, but I'm prepared to make an exception.'

'We had a deal,' Emma said, her voice shaky.

Seb wanted to fling his arms around her. She was petrified and hurting, but still she managed to sound so sure of herself, so defiant.

'Unfortunately I'm not a man of my word,' the bandit said, smiling to reveal yellowed teeth.

Seb was ready to pounce, but something held him back. He knew he only had one opportunity and right now wasn't the time to make his move. He needed all the bandits together, otherwise he wouldn't have a chance. With the anger mounting inside him he forced himself to sit still.

The chief bandit pulled Emma a couple of steps closer to the rest of his men.

'I think you owe us some entertainment for all the trouble you've caused us,' the bandit said.

Emma stood completely still and Seb could see she was shaking.

'Come on, Miss Knight, we haven't got long before the light fades and I'd like to see what I'm getting before the night draws in.'

The other bandits crowded in closer around her and Seb felt his rage almost boil over. Just a few more minutes, he told himself. Whilst they were preoccupied with Emma he started to free himself from his bonds, ignoring the pain as the rope rubbed the skin from his wrists and focussing on getting completely free of the ropes. He knew it would take him a minute or two to escape; he just hoped the bandits wouldn't do much more before he was in a position to pounce.

He glanced up and what he saw made his blood boil in his veins. One of the bandits had grabbed Emma's shirt and was pulling it over her head. Emma was struggling valiantly against him, but this just seemed to amuse her attackers more. Finally they managed to pull the shirt from her head and Emma was left standing with just her chemise covering her top half.

'Such beautiful skin,' the chief bandit said, running a finger across the skin of her shoulders.

Seb watched as Emma tried to squirm away from him, but it was to no avail.

'Now let's see the rest of you.'

With those words Seb felt a red curtain of rage descend over him. No one treated Emma like that. She was precious, to be loved and cherished, not used and discarded by the likes of these filthy bandits. With a strength he didn't know he possessed Seb ripped the remaining ropes from his wrists and sprang forward.

The bandits never had a chance. Seb lashed out with the fury of a goaded lion and the strength of a bear. He punched left and right, catching two of the bandits on the side of the head, but not waiting to watch them fall. The third stared at him with open eyes, his lips moving as if in prayer. Seb prowled forward, then sprang. He pummelled the man again and again, feeling the blood splatter him from the man's split lip and not stopping until the bandit fell in a crumpled heap on the ground.

Seb looked behind him, checking the three

men were incapacitated before he dealt with the leader.

The red curtain had settled over his eyes and Seb felt as though molten lava were flowing through his veins rather than blood. The chief bandit looked at his accomplices so easily taken out by Seb and started to back away. Seb prowled forward. Suddenly the bandit reached out an arm and grabbed Emma by the neck, pulling her in close to him. From the folds of his robes he produced a knife, the blade glinting in light from the setting sun.

Seb paused as the bandit pressed the knife against the unblemished skin of Emma's throat.

'Don't come any closer,' he warned. For the first time in their acquaintance, his voice was shaking.

Seb coldly weighed up his options. He heard Emma's breathing, heavy and panicking, but tried to put her from his mind for a minute. He needed to focus on this bandit; he needed to neutralise him as a threat and punish him for what he had done to Emma.

Suddenly Seb sprang. He leapt through the air and pushed Emma to the ground before grabbing the bandit by the throat. The two men sank to the desert floor, Seb's hands firmly around the bandit's neck. As he squeezed Seb saw the images of Emma tumbling to the ground behind the moving horse and he saw the bandits stripping her of her shirt, and his fingers tightened their grip.

The bandit's eyes were bulging now, his face the colour of a lobster. Seb knew he should release the man, but he couldn't seem to let go. This man had hurt Emma, and he had planned to do so much more.

Just a few more seconds and Seb knew all the life would be gone from him, but still he couldn't release his grip.

'Sebastian.' Emma laid a hand gently on Seb's arm. 'Let go.'

The words were soft but firm and Seb felt the red haze of rage slowly dissipating. His fingers loosened their grip and as he lay the bandit down on the ground he noted the man was still breathing.

He took a few deep breaths to steady himself, wondering what would have happened if Emma hadn't intervened, then he turned to face her.

She was in his arms immediately, pressing her lips against his and burrowing her body into him as if she never wanted to let go. Seb heard her start to sob and he gently stroked her hair, trying to soothe her.

After a minute or so she pulled away and looked at the four bandits lying incapacitated on the ground.

'What should we do with them?' she asked.

Without saying a word Seb went and fetched the rope from the horses and started to tie the four bandits together. He spent a good ten minutes securing them, knowing if any of the men got free he and Emma would be in the same position as before.

As he returned to Emma's side Seb felt a need for intimacy he'd never experienced before. He wanted to hold her, to inhale her scent, to trace his fingers over her soft skin, to memorise every inch of her body. She anchored him, made him feel in control.

Chapter Twenty-Seven

Emma's body was still shaking as Sebastian scooped her up into his arms. Just a few minutes earlier she had been convinced she was about to be raped by the four bandits. Now they were lying trussed together and she was back in the arms of the man she loved.

Sebastian carried her gently away from the bandits, picking up a blanket as he went. When they were far enough away from the bandits, who were still within his line of sight, he laid her onto the blanket.

'I'd better see to them,' he said, his voice gruff.

Emma nodded, trying to hide her disappointment. She knew he was right, he had to deal with the four men who lay trussed together, but she just wanted him to stay by her side, to wrap his arms around her and never let go.

Sebastian must have sensed her longing and after a glance at the four men who still lay incapacitated he lowered himself to the ground so he sat beside her.

'You're safe now,' he said gently as he wrapped his arms around her body and pulled her against his chest.

Emma felt the tears building in her eyes and began sobbing into the dusty material of his shirt. Sebastian let her cry. He stroked her hair and gently kissed her forehead, but he didn't try to stop her from crying.

After a few minutes Emma felt the tears begin to dry up. She'd been petrified when the men had grabbed hold of her and started to strip her. She had wished herself dead rather than endure their molestation, but she had seen no way out of the situation. Then Sebastian had come charging in like a man possessed. Somehow he had freed himself of his constraints and he had raced to her rescue. The first three men had fallen to the ground in such a blur Emma had no idea what had happened. And then the chief bandit had grabbed her.

She realised her hand was stroking the point on her throat where he had held the blade. He hadn't broken the skin, but she could still feel the cold metal pressed up against her throat and the panic that had gone with it.

Emma had looked into Sebastian's eyes at that moment, but it was as if he had hardly seen her. All his energy and focus had been directed towards the man who threatened her life.

'I will never, ever, let anything bad happen to you again,' Sebastian murmured quietly into her ear.

Emma felt some of the tension melt from her body as she sat cradled in the arms of the man she loved. The idea of a lifetime of protection from Sebastian made her feel secure and safe. Slowly Emma lifted her head from where it was cradled against his chest and looked up into his eyes. Sebastian looked troubled and she knew he was concerned about her, but she sensed there was more to it than that.

Before Emma could ask what was bothering him, one of the bandits started to groan as he came round from unconsciousness.

Gently Sebastian brushed a kiss against her lips and stood, motioning for Emma to stay where she was.

Emma nearly complied. She didn't want to spend any more time in the company of the bandits than she had to, but equally she knew she had to face them, to show them they hadn't broken her spirit. Slowly she stood, her injured ankle protesting and the scrapes on her legs stinging as the material of her trousers brushed against them. Carefully she picked her way towards the men, making sure she remained out of reach all the time.

Sebastian shot her a concerned look, but didn't insist she move away. He must have sensed she needed to confront them.

Two out of four of the men were now conscious. They were the two bandits Sebastian had attacked first. They had got away relatively lightly, both just receiving punches to the head to incapacitate them. The third man lay still on the ground. He was still breathing but his lips had already begun to swell and both his eyes blacken from the punches Sebastian had rained down on him. The chief bandit was breathing evenly but hadn't woken yet.

'What are we going to do with them?' Emma asked.

The two conscious bandits looked at Sebastian for the answer, wanting to know their fate.

'We should just leave them here to die,' Sebastian said.

Emma frowned, knowing she couldn't have that on her conscience.

'They would have done much worse to us.'

She waited for Sebastian to continue.

'But maybe we should give them a sporting chance.'

'Please have mercy,' one of the conscious men said in stilted English. 'I have a family, children.'

Emma wondered if it was true or whether the bandit was merely saying it to try and save his skin.

As Sebastian contemplated what to do with the men the chief bandit began to stir, and a minute later the final man regained consciousness. Initially both men strained against their bonds but it was to no avail.

'Where is Miss Knight's scroll?' Sebastian asked once all four men were completely awake.

At first it looked as though the chief bandit might refuse to answer, but after a few seconds he must have seen how pointless it would be to put up any kind of futile resistance.

'In the pocket of my robe.'

Cautiously Sebastian bent down and plucked the scroll from the bandit's robe. He handed it back to Emma. She ran her fingers over the familiar grooves in the papyrus and smiled weakly at Sebastian. She just wanted this to be over with.

'Let my companions go,' the chief bandit said after a few minutes of silence. 'They have families, people who rely on them.'

Sebastian didn't move. 'And they were quite happy to abduct, rape and kill Miss Knight. Having a family is not a saving grace.'

Emma watched as the three men stared resolutely at the ground.

'Answer all my questions honestly and I will think about letting them go,' Sebastian said.

The chief bandit nodded.

'Who else knows you are here?'

'My brother, Hanif. He urged me not to come on this mission.'

'Anyone else?'

The bandit shook his head.

'I wanted to restore our family honour, to take back what had been so wrongfully stolen from us.'

Sebastian looked at him coldly. 'And hurting an innocent woman helps to restore your family's honour?' he asked, shaking his head.

Before the bandit had a chance to answer Emma stepped forward.

'How did you know I had the scroll?'

The question had been bugging her since she'd first set eyes on the bandit in her room at the Fitzgeralds'. She hadn't advertised the fact she carried a scroll that held the secret of the location of a long-lost tomb.

'I was just a child when the scroll was lost to your father. But I vowed one day to get it back, to restore our family's honour. For years it was out of my reach, but I kept my ears open. When I heard your name, the fact that you'd arrived in Cairo, I knew you must have the scroll with you. And why else would you hire someone like Mr Oakfield to take you out into the desert?'

'Tell me your names,' Sebastian demanded, 'and I'll know if you lie.'

After a few seconds of debate the chief bandit recited four names. They were long Arabic names, but Emma could see Sebastian had memorised them easily.

'What will you do to us?' the chief bandit asked, no hint of fear in his voice, just resignation.

Sebastian ignored the question and Emma watched as he silently went to work retying the knots that secured the bandits. By the time he was finished they all had their hands tied behind their backs and were secured to one another via a rope around the neck. It meant they would be able to walk along in a line, one behind the other.

Slowly Sebastian went along the line and gave each bandit a long drink of water from the water skin.

'Enjoy,' he said. 'This is the last water you'll have for a while.'

'Please,' one of the bandits said in heavily accented English. 'Have mercy.'

'I am,' Sebastian said with a stony expression. 'This is much more than you deserve.'

Emma realised what he was planning. He would let the bandits go, but he was going to make them suffer for what they had planned to do to her.

Sebastian then pointed in the direction that they'd come. 'Walk for two days in that direction and you'll reach a small village called Behpe. I'm sure they will release you there.'

'We will never survive for two days without water.'

Sebastian gave them a hard look. 'I have been in the desert for three days without water before and I'm still here. And honestly if you don't

survive, it won't cause me any sleepless nights.
Now go before I change my mind.'

Still they didn't move.

Sebastian quickly recited all their names and
gave each man a stony look.

'I'd get moving if I were you. And remember if I ever hear that you've caused any trouble, if you so much as hurt an insect and it gets
back to my ears, I'll inform the authorities and
you'll all spend the rest of your lives behind
bars or worse.'

This seemed to galvanise the four men into
action. Slowly they started to move, glancing to
where their horses were tethered, knowing there
was no way Sebastian would give the beasts to
them for their journey.

'Will they survive?' Emma asked. She hated
them for what they had planned to do to her and
Sebastian, but she didn't want their deaths on
her conscience.

Sebastian nodded. 'Behpe is only just over
ten hours' walk from here. They'll be parched
when they arrive, but they'll survive.'

They both watched as the four men became
smaller and smaller as they moved farther away.
When they were mere silhouettes on the hori-

zon Sebastian turned to Emma and looked her over with concern.

'Will you recover?' he asked.

Emma nodded. Her legs hurt and her ankle ached and she'd been more scared than she'd ever been in her life, but she would survive.

'Thank you for saving me,' she whispered quietly.

Sebastian smiled as if her words amused him.

'I thought I was going to lose you,' he said eventually. Emma heard the catch in his voice and saw the look of pain on his face.

'But you didn't,' she said, moving closer to him.

'I didn't.'

Silently he raised his hand and began to trace the contours of her face with his fingers. With a groan he pulled her towards him and kissed her deeply. She felt his arms hold her tightly against his body and felt the pent-up energy radiating from him.

Slowly they broke off their kiss and Sebastian spent a minute just looking at her. Then, unexpectedly, he scooped her up into his arms and strode to where he'd placed the blanket earlier. Gently he laid her on her back and Emma felt a thrill of anticipation as he positioned his body over hers.

In the light from the dying sun Emma could see an urgency about him she'd never witnessed before. He looked as though he wanted to savour every memory because it might be his last. Then he lowered his lips to hers and she forgot everything else.

He kissed her gently at first, as though he thought he might injure her, but she could feel the desire breaking through and soon his kiss was all-consuming. Emma writhed underneath him as he ran his hands over her body and she felt her hips buck up to meet his.

Suddenly he stopped and pulled away and Emma felt empty and alone without the weight of his body on top of hers.

'Your legs,' he rasped.

She glanced down at her legs, wondering what he meant.

Gently he began to remove her ripped trousers, peeling them from her body and inspecting what was underneath.

'Your poor beautiful legs,' Sebastian murmured.

Emma glanced down. She'd never thought of her legs as beautiful before.

The grazes on her knees and lower legs were already beginning to scab over and the stinging had much improved, but they looked dreadful.

Sebastian held each leg up in the air and inspected it. Emma couldn't help but giggle.

'Satisfactory?' she asked, trying to keep a straight face.

'I should have killed them for what they did to you.'

'It's just a few scrapes,' Emma said soothingly. 'I'll heal within a few days and it'll be like it never happened.'

Sebastian grimaced and Emma knew she had to stop the thoughts that were running through his head. He was blaming himself for what had happened. Even though he'd been the one to save her.

Gently she reached up and laced her fingers around his neck and pulled him back down with her. Sebastian resisted at first, then groaned and surrendered. He peppered kisses along the angle of her jaw and down her neck and soon Emma was writhing with pleasure and all her injuries were completely forgotten.

Wordlessly Sebastian pulled away, just long enough to lift her chemise and underwear from her body. He looked at her for a minute and

Emma just lay there, basking in his attention. She knew she should feel shy or bashful, but Sebastian made her proud of her body. He made her want to strip off in front of him and encourage his perusal of her curves.

Silently she reached up and cupped his face with her hand, wanting to memorise every detail of his face. For a few seconds they looked deep into each other's eyes and then his lips were back on hers.

This time there was an urgency about his kiss, as if he'd remembered he'd nearly lost her and was trying to banish that memory. Emma knew she was also trying to forget, to replace the awful events from the day with images only of Sebastian.

She reached up and started tugging at the waistband of his trousers, wanting to feel his skin against hers. Frantically Sebastian pulled his shirt over his head and pushed his trousers off and finally there was nothing between them but the warm desert air.

Sebastian paused for a second, poised above her, as if savouring the moment, then he lowered his body on top of hers.

Emma gasped when he entered her. Unlike the last time they'd made love there was no gentle start, but with one thrust Sebastian was completely inside her. Emma felt full and safe and completed. She grabbed hold of him as he tried to pull out and held him still for a few seconds longer, enjoying the sensation of being one with Sebastian. Then her desire got the better of her and her hips started to buck. Her body met each and every thrust and they seemed to move as one. Sebastian kissed her as he thrust into her and muffled Emma's moans of pleasure.

After only a minute Emma felt the pleasure building up inside her and knew she was about to climax. As the waves of pleasure washed over her she felt her muscles clench, but still Sebastian continued to thrust. Then it was his turn, and she felt him explode inside her with a soft groan.

Gently he rolled off her and pulled her body to him. Emma couldn't help but smile. Despite what they'd been through it was the perfect finish to the day. Their lovemaking might not have been the slow, unhurried perusal of each other's bodies that they'd enjoyed the previous night, but it had been exactly what they'd both needed. And now she was in Sebastian's arms and the world felt right again.

Emma must have slept, although she couldn't

remember her eyes growing heavy or her body beginning to relax. When she awoke the sun was just starting to rise over the horizon. She felt warm and safe and happy and realised that was mainly because Sebastian was still sleeping behind her with his arm looped around her body. Contentedly she nestled into him and enjoyed the moment.

After a few minutes Sebastian began to stir and Emma turned to face him.

'Good morning,' she said, planting a kiss gently on his lips.

Sebastian frowned and glanced around him, as if trying to piece together the events from the night before.

Slowly he sat up and stretched, causing the blanket he'd placed over them as they slept to fall down a little.

Emma saw his gaze travel down to her breasts and she smiled, edging in closer.

Sebastian coughed and quickly reached for his clothes.

'We'd better pack up the camp,' he said, his voice gruff.

Emma nodded, trying to hide her disappointment. She knew he was right, now wasn't the time to be amorous, but she didn't like how uncomfortable he seemed. Surely after all that had happened he knew she loved him. And she was pretty sure he loved her as well. He hadn't said as much, but there was no mistaking the way he looked at her and how fiercely he'd fought to protect her. Surely she couldn't be wrong?

Reluctantly Emma pulled on her clothes, wincing as the fabric of her trousers brushed against first her injured ankle and then the grazes on her legs. They both dressed in silence and Emma self-consciously ran a hand through her hair before turning back to face Sebastian.

She could see the longing in his eyes and knew he wanted nothing more than to walk over and take her in his arms, but something was holding him back.

Emma wanted to reach out to him, find out what was wrong, but she was afraid what the answer might be. After spending another night in his arms she knew she had weaved a fantasy life with Sebastian at its centre, and if she had to find out that wasn't going to happen she didn't know how she would cope.

Chapter Twenty-Eight

Seb saw the way Emma was looking at him but he knew he couldn't cope with her questions right now. So instead he busied himself packing up the camp and readying them for their journey to Luxor.

'I'm not turning back,' Emma said suddenly, 'if that's your plan.'

Of course it was his plan. After everything she'd been through Emma was mad if she thought Seb would let her continue on this trek through the desert following a scroll that might still turn out to be a fake.

'We need to get you to a doctor.'

Emma snorted. 'I've got a few grazes. I'm sure I'll live.'

'They could become infected.'

She raised her eyebrows. 'I'm not turning

back now, otherwise this would have all been for nothing.'

Seb studied her for a few seconds, saw the serious expression on her face and knew he wouldn't get her to change her mind. He could just fling her over his shoulder and carry her back to Luxor, but after her treatment of the last few days he doubted she would go without a fight.

He sighed and ran a hand through his hair.

'We should reach the spot on the scroll by nightfall. If we haven't found anything by dusk tomorrow we turn back.'

Emma's face split into a huge grin and for a second Seb thought she might throw herself into his arms. Then she tensed slightly and instead backed away a step or two.

Silently Seb finished loading the horses. He helped Emma onto Wadjet then tied the bandits' horses in a line together and secured them to his horse before mounting.

For a while they rode in silence. Seb could see Emma flicking glances his way every few seconds, obviously trying to figure out why he was acting so coldly towards her. He didn't want to, in fact he hated himself a little for what he was putting her through, but it was probably for the best.

Seb knew after making love to Emma twice he would have to marry her. Part of him was filled with joy and happiness at the thought. He loved Emma. He'd realised it when he'd seen her fall to her knees behind the bandit's horse and he'd felt part of his heart die with worry. He loved her and he would marry her, but that didn't mean they could have a future together.

Seb knew he would have to send her away. He could send her back to England as his wife. It would break his heart to do it, but it was better than the alternative. It was better than her staying with him and one day being on the receiving end of one of his rages.

The night before, when the bandit had ripped Emma's shirt off, he'd seen red. He hadn't been in control of his body or his actions. His instincts had taken over and he'd sprung. And he knew if Emma hadn't been there, telling him to stop, he would have killed that man. It made him feel sick inside. What scared him even more was how little control he'd had over his body.

He shook his head. There was no way he

could ever risk Emma being in that situation. Sending her away would break his heart, but at least she would be safe from him.

He glanced over at her, looking at her profile and the blank expression on her face, and he knew she would survive. She was strong and brave, and, although she probably wouldn't understand his reasons, she would be all right in the end. She might hate him for sending her away, but she was a survivor, and eventually she would find her own happiness. It would just be Seb who was left in a never-ending cycle of self-hatred and guilt.

'We should talk,' Seb said quietly, wondering how best to break the news to her.

He knew she loved him, or at least knew she thought she loved him. Telling her he would marry her but they couldn't stay together would break her heart.

Emma looked at him warily but nodded all the same.

'Last night,' Seb started, then paused, unsure how to go on.

'Last night was lovely,' Emma said.

Seb nodded, knowing he had to take control of the conversation but not sure how.

'Sebastian,' Emma said, her eyes filling with

tears, 'before you say any more I want you to know I love you.'

Seb felt the lump in his throat grow as he tried to find the words to respond. He knew telling her he loved her with all his heart would only give her the wrong idea, but now was the time for honesty, otherwise she would never understand his reasoning.

'I think I've loved you from the moment we shared that kiss on the terrace,' Seb said, realising it was true. All this time he'd been trying to deny it because he knew they couldn't have a future together.

Emma's expression transformed from worry to pure happiness.

'Oh, Sebastian, you don't know—'

He had to cut her off. He held up a hand and shook his head.

'I love you, Emma. And we should marry, but we can't be together.'

She looked as though he'd just slapped her.

'But if we love each other and we marry then we will be together.'

Seb hated that he was responsible for the tears that sprang to her eyes. He just wanted to scoop her up into his arms and gallop off into the horizon.

'We can't be together,' he repeated.

Emma fell silent and just looked at him and Seb felt his words leave him. How was he meant to tell this wonderful woman he would send her back to England after the formalities of a marriage ceremony?

'I'm not safe,' he said eventually.

Emma actually laughed. 'Of course you're safe, Sebastian. I know you'd never hurt me.'

'You can't know that. No one can know that.'

'I know that. I know that you love me and I know you wouldn't hurt someone you loved.'

'Emma, I can't take that risk. You'll be safer without me—happier, too.'

Fiercely she wiped the tears away from her cheeks and rounded on him. 'Don't tell me what would make me happier. If you think sending me away, discarding me, would make me happy then you don't know me at all.'

Seb wished he could just pull her into his arms and kiss all the pain and hurt away, but he knew after this conversation they would never be intimate again. He felt a stab of anguish in his heart at the thought and wondered when holding Emma close to his chest had become the most important thing in his life.

'If you don't love me and don't want me then

I'd prefer it if you didn't pretend otherwise. I know men just use women and then throw them away. Don't feel like you have to dress this up differently.'

Seb knew she had to lash out but when she did it caught him unawares. He wanted to protest his love for her, tell her she mattered more than water and sunlight and air, but he knew that would only confuse matters more.

'Emma, you know that isn't the issue,' he said.

'You say you love me...' the tears were back now and her voice had become thick with emotion '...but I love you and I know I wouldn't give you up without a fight.'

'When that bandit ripped your shirt off I couldn't control myself,' Seb said, hoping if he could explain properly she might understand. 'I would have killed him if it wasn't for you.'

'But you didn't. You stopped. Anyway, I think any man could be forgiven for beating someone who was trying to rape the woman they supposedly love.'

'I lost control, Emma, and I've lost control before. I can't guarantee that I won't lose control with you one day.'

'Then let me be the one willing to take that risk, because I know you would never hurt me.'

Seb shook his head. 'No.'

At his blunt reply Emma recoiled so much Seb wondered whether she might fall off her horse, but she regained her balance and kept her seat.

'So what do you propose?' she asked, her voice emotionless.

'We marry when we return to Cairo, then you travel back to England.'

'To live as a woman whose husband has sent her continents away? No, thank you.'

Seb looked at her but she refused to meet his gaze.

'It's the only way.'

'If you insist on sending me away then we won't marry. There's no point.'

Seb felt a cold panic inside his chest. He had counted on marrying Emma, on always having that tie to her. If she returned a single woman to England he would lose her completely and all they had shared would just be a memory.

'You might be with child,' he said quickly.

Emma shrugged. 'Equally I might not.'

'We can't take that chance. I wouldn't want you to go through a scandal like that.'

She turned to him with disbelief in her eyes. 'But you don't mind sending me and your unborn child to fend for ourselves in England, never to see you again.'

Seb felt his world fall apart. She could be pregnant; it was a definite possibility. And she was right: if she was pregnant he would be sending her to raise his child alone, and he'd never see them.

'I'll stay in Cairo until we can be sure I'm not pregnant,' Emma said wearily.

Seb turned to look at her. She looked ashen, broken. He hated that he was the one doing this to her. All he wanted was to spend eternity holding her and kissing her and showering her with love. Instead he was destroying her.

'It'll be for the best, Emma.'

She shook her head. 'You can tell yourself that but I don't believe it for one second. We will both be miserable and alone for the rest of our lives, when we have the opportunity to be happy. All for a precaution, for something that will never happen.'

He wished she were right, but Seb thought back to the previous night and the rage that had fallen upon him. He couldn't risk Emma ever being on the other end of that, even if it meant breaking both their hearts.

Chapter Twenty-Nine

They'd ridden for three hours in silence before stopping for lunch, and since dismounting Emma had stopped any of Sebastian's attempts at starting a conversation with a stony glare. She didn't want to make small talk or discuss the ending of their journey; all she wanted was for Sebastian to throw his arms around her and admit he was wrong.

Emma understood his concerns, but that didn't mean she agreed with them. She understood that on occasion he found it difficult to control his temper, but from what she'd seen and his story about his father, both had been very exact circumstances. In both cases he'd lost his temper when someone was threatening a person he cared for. Many men would react in the same way. He'd never laid a finger on her—well, not in a violent fashion anyway, and Emma believed she knew him well enough to be sure that he wouldn't.

She wished she could somehow make him see how happy their life would be together. She knew he loved her, she could see it in his eyes, and she knew it was breaking his heart to send her away. But Sebastian was a stubborn man, and he'd got it into his head that if they built a life together he would end up hurting her. Maybe not in a week or a year, but eventually.

Emma wondered if she should just accept his wishes and return to England. She glanced at Sebastian and saw the unhappiness in his eyes and she knew she wasn't going to give him up without a fight. This last couple of weeks had been the happiest of her life, despite the hardships of the desert and despite being kidnapped by bandits. Sebastian was the reason she had enjoyed herself so much, and she was planning on building on that happiness for the rest of their lives.

Sebastian handed her a fresh water skin and a handful of dried fruit. As his hand touched hers it seemed as though he set her on fire. Emma caught hold of his fingers before he pulled away. She tugged on his arm until he relented and sat down next to her.

'I won't marry you if you plan on sending me back to England,' Emma said, 'and I'm planning on staying in Cairo for the foreseeable future, but that doesn't have to be as your wife.'

Sebastian looked at her, confused.

'In fact you wouldn't have to see me at all,' Emma said sadly.

She knew it would be torture remaining in Cairo, knowing she could bump into Sebastian at any moment, but if it was torture for her then it would be torture for him as well.

'Emma, you know that's a bad idea.'

Calmly she raised her eyebrows. 'As bad an idea as destroying both our chances for happiness for something that will never happen?'

Sebastian opened his mouth to protest but Emma held up her hand to silence him.

'You've said your bit, Sebastian, now I want you to listen to me.'

She waited until he clamped his lips firmly together and nodded.

'Since meeting you my life has changed. I never knew how unhappy I was. I was destined to spend my life alone, and then I met you.' Emma reached up and ran her fingers over his cheek. 'You made me realise I could be loved and you made me fall head over heels in love with you.'

Emma couldn't help herself, she leaned forward and gently kissed him on the lips.

'You are a good man, Sebastian, one of the best, and I think it must have been dreadful to go through what you did in your childhood, but you can't let that ruin the rest of your life.'

Emma paused again and looked deep into Sebastian's eyes.

'You're not your father.'

Sebastian opened his mouth to speak but Emma shook her head. 'I haven't finished yet. I love you. I love you, Sebastian, and I'm willing to do whatever it takes to make you realise we can have a life together. So I won't be running back to England when we return to Cairo. I won't make it that easy for you.'

She leant forward again and brushed another feather-light kiss across his lips. Sebastian responded, trying to pull her deeper into the kiss but Emma pulled back.

'You've got a lot to think about,' she said, standing up and stretching.

Silently she allowed Sebastian to help her remount Wadjet. She noticed when his fingers caressed her leg for just a moment longer than was necessary and she saw how he kept glancing at her. She knew internally he was in turmoil, she could see he didn't want to lose her, but the years of telling himself he was too dangerous to be with a woman wouldn't fade away that quickly. She only hoped he changed his mind before it was too late.

Sebastian consulted the scroll before they set off.

'Should only take us about four more hours,' he said quietly.

Emma nodded, wondering where her enthusiasm for their treasure hunt had gone. If Sebastian wasn't holding her hand as they entered the tomb was it all really worth it? A few weeks ago she would have chosen an Ancient Egyptian tomb over love any day, but now she would sacrifice discovering a hundred tombs for just one more day of bliss with Sebastian.

About an hour before sunset the terrain started to change. Instead of the undulating sand dunes or rocky desert floor there began to be small outcrops of rock. As they rode further these turned into larger rocky cliffs and mounds, just the perfect place to conceal a royal tomb.

'We're not all that far from the tombs of the

pharaohs discovered near Luxor,' Sebastian commented.

Emma glanced at him and saw the first spark of excitement in his eyes. She looked up at the cliffs and wondered what treasures they concealed within their depths.

Sebastian stopped his horse and consulted the scroll once more.

'We're looking for a place where two cliffs come together as if they were kissing,' he said confidently.

They continued on for a few minutes before Emma spotted it.

'There,' she said, her voice barely a whisper.

Nearly half a mile up ahead two cliffs leaned inwards towards each other, the tops of the cliffs so close you could imagine them kissing.

With renewed energy they spurred their horses forward. Emma glanced at the sky. They only had about half an hour of good light left. She knew they wouldn't find the tomb today, but maybe they might see something, some clue that this whole expedition hadn't been for nothing.

As they drew closer the cliffs looked just like any other. From this distance there wasn't anything that set them apart, that advertised the fact there could be a royal tomb hidden inside, but Emma knew deep down that they were in the right place.

She tried to imagine what it had been like two thousand years ago when these tombs were being built, wondered whether the pharaohs and queens had thought their final resting places would hold such fascination for the people of the future.

Sebastian signalled for them to stop.

'We should make camp here and start our search in the morning. We don't want to miss anything.'

Despite Emma's wish to start their search now she knew what Sebastian said made sense. They were likely to miss small details in the fading light and she knew they didn't have much time. It would make more sense to start afresh in the morning and not have to cover the same ground twice.

Silently they started to set up their camp. Emma laid out the sleeping mats and blankets, placing them side by side. She didn't know if Sebastian would move his later, but if this was to be one of their last nights together she wanted him close by. There wasn't anything to build a fire from so they ate the last of the flat bread and some more dried fruit. Emma supposed she would enjoy eating her first real meal for two weeks in a couple of days' time, but if staying in the desert meant putting off separating from Sebastian she would be happy to live on dried meat and stale bread for her entire life.

'We should get some rest. We'll have a long day of searching tomorrow,' Sebastian said. It was his first attempt at communicating with her since they'd stopped riding. He looked troubled and had frowned into his simple meal as he ate. Emma knew she had done everything she could to persuade him they were meant to be together; now he had to make up his own mind.

Emma stretched out underneath her blanket and looked up at the sky. She'd miss seeing the stars before she went to sleep when they returned to civilisation.

Sebastian lay down next to her, his body so close she could reach out an arm and touch him, yet seeming so far away.

After a few minutes Emma knew sleep wouldn't come easily. She turned over to face Sebastian, his features indistinguishable in the darkness.

'Sebastian,' Emma said quietly, 'if this is going to be one of our last nights together, will you hold me?'

For a minute he didn't move, and Emma had a horrible sinking feeling that he might refuse. Then she heard him shuffle closer. They lay face to face, his breath tickling her cheeks. Emma reached out and placed a hand on his chest, feeling the thud of his heart through his skin. Sebastian looped his arm around Emma's waist, pulling her even closer to him. They were completely entwined, their two bodies now as one. Emma felt the tears start to roll down her cheeks but didn't move to brush them away. She was going to make the most of this night; if they were to go their separate ways she was determined she would always have these memories to sustain her.

Slowly Emma felt herself relax. She hadn't thought she would sleep at all, but here, in Sebastian's arms, momentarily everything seemed right again.

Chapter Thirty

Seb awoke with the dawn. His arm was still looped around Emma's waist and her head had fallen to nestle into his shoulder. He took a few minutes to memorise how she looked when she slept; he wanted his memories to last for ever.

She stirred a little but did not wake and Seb wondered if it would be easier if he pulled away. Although he knew looking into her eyes before she remembered all that had passed between them would be exquisitely painful, he just couldn't bring himself to move. This could be the last time he ever held her. That thought broke his heart all over again.

He wondered if she was right, if he was doing all of this unnecessarily. Maybe they could live happily together, spend their lives loving each other. Maybe all his precautions were completely unnecessary. Then he pictured the bandit's bloody face and he knew he just couldn't take that risk.

'Good morning,' Emma said dozily as her eyes fluttered open.

'Good morning.' Seb couldn't help but smile. She looked so beautiful in the soft morning light.

'You're lovely and warm,' Emma said, her eyes still not properly open. Seb felt her burrow in closer to him, pressing her entire body up against his. She wriggled, trying to get comfortable, and he felt her brush up against him. Softly Seb groaned.

Emma looked at him for a second before understanding dawned in her eyes. Gently she brushed against him again.

'Emma,' he said, trying to make his voice stern.

'Yes, Sebastian?' she said lightly.

'We can't.'

She didn't stop and Seb felt his resolve weaken.

'Emma,' he repeated again.

This time she ignored him and moved one hand under the blankets.

Seb groaned. He knew he should roll away.

He knew any intimacy between them would just complicate matters even further. But somehow he just couldn't seem to bring himself to push her away.

Emma nestled farther into his neck and started to plant soft kisses just below his ear. Suddenly she caught his earlobe in her mouth and gently began to suck.

'Emma,' Seb groaned, not knowing whether he was begging her to continue or pleading with her to stop.

'Shh,' she said, pulling away slightly. 'This doesn't change anything. It just leaves us with a memory to treasure for ever.'

Seb's resolve buckled and he found himself kissing her back with such fervour he hoped he wouldn't scare her away. Emma responded with passion of her own, running her hands all over his body, but always returning to the hardness of his manhood straining beneath his trousers.

He felt her tug at his shirt and obligingly Seb lifted his arms up so she could pull it over his head. For a second Emma just stared at his torso, as if really trying to commit every detail of him to memory. Seb felt a stab of panic. This couldn't be the last time he was with Emma; surely there had to be more.

Emma pushed him back towards the ground and swiftly climbed on top of him, straddling his hips. He felt her lower herself on top of his hardness and groaned as she wriggled around for a few seconds.

'Clothes off,' he gasped, wanting to see her naked, wanting to touch every inch of her skin.

Emma grinned and started to tug off her shirt and chemise. He reached up and cupped her breasts in both hands, causing her to drop her head back and writhe in pleasure. Softly he caressed the milky white skin then caught both her nipples between his fingers and rolled them ever so gently backwards and forwards.

Emma responded by lifting her hips and trying to tug down his trousers, but Sebastian had other ideas. He propped himself up on his elbows and started to loosen her trousers, racing to see if he could undress her first.

He won, pulling her trousers down over her hips and waiting as she lifted herself off her knees and out of the garment. Finally she was naked atop him and Seb took a moment to just admire her. She was beautiful and strong and proud. He couldn't believe just a couple of weeks ago he'd never even met her. It seemed as though they'd known each other for a lifetime.

Slowly he trailed his fingers down between her breasts and over the taut muscles of her abdomen. He paused momentarily before he reached the soft curls at the bottom of her abdomen, then dipped even lower. Emma gasped with pleasure as his fingers gently circled and probed and he felt her buck against him.

'This isn't fair,' Emma said, barely able to catch her breath.

Seb ignored her, instead focussing on the movement of his fingers and the rise and fall of her chest as she panted.

'You're still half clothed,' she managed to get out.

Obligingly Seb paused and lifted his hips to allow Emma to pull off his trousers. Then it was his turn to groan with surprise as she caught him between her hands and started to stroke.

'Emma,' he said, his voice low with desire.

'Yes, Sebastian?'

'Don't stop.'

She smiled and he felt her grip tighten. His hips bucked up involuntarily as he felt her fingers glide over his skin, backwards and forwards, over and over again.

Seb knew he had to have her soon, and so he grabbed her hips and positioned her over him.

Slowly she lowered herself until he was just about to enter her.

'Maybe we should stop,' she said teasingly.

'No. Never.'

With gentle pressure he pushed her downwards and sighed as he felt himself slip inside her. Slowly Emma began rocking, picking up the pace as she flung her head back and started to moan with pleasure.

He watched her above him and he knew he would never love anyone as he loved her. She was his one and only; she was the woman who completed him.

Seb felt the climax build inside him and pulled her forward onto his chest. Emma tightened around him as he exploded inside her and then they lay panting together, neither wanting to be the one to move and spoil the moment.

'Thank you for that,' Emma said as she lifted her head and looked in his eyes.

Seb didn't know what to say.

'I wanted one last memory of us together.'

He wrapped his arms tightly around her and held her close to his chest. He didn't want this to be his last memory of her. He wanted to make a lifetime of memories with her. He wanted to wake up every morning with her in his arms and he wanted to take her on his adventures during the day. And then each and every evening he wanted to make love to her before falling asleep with the woman he loved wrapped tightly in his embrace.

Maybe it is possible, a small voice said inside his head. Maybe you can have all that and more? He thought about the future they would have together. Saturdays spent ambling round the streets of Cairo, arm in arm, and long Sundays spent in bed with no one else to disturb them.

Maybe even children. Seb had never imagined himself having children, but with Emma he could see it so clearly. They'd have beautiful little girls with blond hair and blue eyes, the perfect miniature of their lovely mother.

He shook his head. Surely it wasn't possible? Surely it was just all a fantasy?

'We should get started,' Emma said, breaking the moment.

Seb nodded, knowing they needed to start the day, but wanting to lie for just a little longer with Emma pressed against his heart.

She wriggled for a few seconds then stopped and looked at him when she realised he wasn't about to release her.

'I can't get dressed with you holding me like this,' she said.

Seb didn't move.

'You gave me until dusk to find the tomb,' Emma continued, 'so we need to get moving.'

Seb cursed himself for his rash imposition of a time restriction. Why hadn't he said they could stay out in the desert for weeks? Here it was just the two of them; they could easily be together. As soon as they returned to civilisation he would have to give Emma up for good. Maybe he could just kidnap her and wander off into the desert with her slung over his horse?

Seb stopped in his tracks. It was only him who was stopping them from being together. If he said the word he knew Emma would never leave his side again.

He shook his head and loosened his grip on Emma, allowing her to roll off him and start pulling on her clothes. He was doing this to protect her, to make sure she never came to any harm.

Reluctantly Seb started to dress as well and soon they were packing away their camp and ready to start their search.

'How shall we go about it?' Emma asked as they both sat looking at the scroll.

Seb leaned in closer than was strictly necessary on the pretence of studying the scroll and stayed there for a few seconds.

'The entrance will be hidden,' he said. 'That was the whole point of building the tombs out in the middle of the desert, but it will be marked in some way.'

He contemplated for a few seconds.

'We should take a cliff face each and spend time really studying the rock, seeing if there is anything that could be interpreted as a symbol. Remember it will be worn down after all these years exposed to the elements.'

Emma nodded.

'If we get to the end of these rock faces we'll swap places and double back. I'm pretty sure we're in the right vicinity. It'll be finding the exact spot that will be difficult.'

Emma stood and stretched. She picked up her water skin and regarded the two rock faces.

'Do you want the left or the right?' she asked.

Seb shrugged, allowing her to pick. Emma started on the left. She walked up to the rock face and began studying it in earnest. Seb watched her for a few seconds before walking over to the opposite side of the ravine.

Every few minutes he would pause and look

over to where Emma was slowly making progress. She was loving every second; he could tell by the look on her face. He'd never thought he'd find someone who loved Egyptology as much as he did, but here she was—the perfect woman had fallen right into his arms.

Seb tried to concentrate on the rock face, but thoughts of Emma kept entering his mind. He couldn't allow the next couple of days to be their last together. There must be some way of keeping her safe but still keeping her with him. He'd give anything to know he would never harm her.

Seb traced his fingers over the rock and tried to pick out any man-made markings. Often touch was the best way to pick something up. Nature didn't often leave completely straight lines, so if he ran his fingers over a rock and found one then that could be the clue they needed.

He thought he should share this pearl of wisdom with Emma so quickly strode over to her.

'Have you found something?' Emma asked, her voice high with excitement.

He shook his head. 'I thought I'd just say use your fingers.'

Emma's eyes widened and then she giggled.

'On the rock,' Seb said, keeping his face completely serious. 'You might pick up something that your eyes can't see.'

Emma saluted him then turned back to the rock. Seb lingered for a few seconds longer, wondering whether it would be bad form to reach out, spin her round and kiss her.

He sighed, and reached out. When it came to Emma it seemed his common sense left him.

Gently he spun her round, planted a firm kiss on her lips and then walked off, knowing she would be wondering what it meant and knowing he couldn't tell her.

They continued their search, edging along the rock face as the sun climbed ever higher in the sky. At the beginning of the day Seb had been convinced they would find the tomb, but now he wasn't so sure. They were almost three quarters of the way along the rock face and so far they had found no clue whatsoever.

'Sebastian,' Emma called, breaking Seb from his trance.

Quickly he spun round and picked his way across the rough ground to where Emma was standing. She had stepped back from the rock face a little and was looking up to a spot somewhere above her head.

'What is it?' he asked, peering upwards, trying to shield his eyes from the glaring sun.

'I think we've found it,' Emma said, taking his hand in hers. 'I think we've found the entrance to the tomb.'

Chapter Thirty-One

Sebastian peered up at the rock face as Emma pointed to the spot that had caught her attention. Her interest had been piqued as she'd seen the rock face seemed to be eroded back into a crevice above ground level and there was a ledge just above her head leading to it. So she'd stepped back and studied the area for a while. And then she'd seen it. The small carving, now eroded by the wind and sand of the desert, but still recognisable as some sort of bird of prey.

She watched as Sebastian's eyes alighted upon it and his whole face transformed into a smile.

'That's it,' he said. 'That's got to be it.'

Emma's breath caught in her throat as he reached out and took her hand. For a second they just stood there, hand in hand, looking up at the small carving.

'How will we get up there?' Emma asked as she eyed the surrounding rock face.

'You can pull me up,' Sebastian quipped and Emma caught a glimpse of the carefree man she'd travelled with until their encounter with the bandits. Sebastian quickly studied the terrain, then motioned for her to wait where she was. He dashed back the way they'd come, leaving Emma wondering what he had planned.

After a couple of minutes he returned with two large sticks wrapped in cloth. He threw them up onto the ledge above their heads and ran his hands over the rock.

'If I boost you up do you think you'll have the strength to pull yourself the rest of the way?' he asked.

Emma judged the distance then nodded. 'But how will you get up there? It's a long way without someone to boost you.'

'Don't worry. I wouldn't miss this for the world.'

Emma crossed the couple of steps to where Sebastian was standing and flexed her fingers. When she was ready she put her booted foot into Sebastian's hand. He pushed upwards and Emma found herself soaring towards the sky so her chest was level with the ledge. Without too much effort she managed to pull herself the rest of the way onto the ledge. She scooted back from the edge and watched as Sebastian tested out various bits of the rock face. He quickly decided on a route and within a couple of seconds he had pulled himself up and was sitting beside her.

Hand in hand they stood and moved towards the small carving. Emma reached out her fingers and traced the outline. Up close it was unmistakable; this was definitely a man-made carving.

Sebastian led her back to where the ledge narrowed into a V shape, with a crevice leading further in. Emma gasped as he released her hand and squeezed around the rock face, only to disappear completely from view.

'Come on in,' Sebastian said, his voice echoing slightly.

With a glance back over her shoulder Emma squeezed herself round the rock face and followed him. To her surprise the ledge widened out again and in the middle of the cliff at the back was a doorway. She looked back the way they had come and saw they were completely hidden from view.

She felt a shiver run through her body. There

was a possibility they were the first people to lay eyes on this entrance for thousands of years.

Sebastian quickly retreated the way they'd come and picked up the as-yet-unlit torches. He spent a couple of minutes building a small fire and coaxing a flame to light the rags before setting one aflame and handing it to Emma. He took the other one in his free hand.

'Shall we?' he asked. 'Or shall we just go home now we've found it?'

Emma nodded, answering his first question and ignoring his second. She sensed he was nervous and she felt the same. Her throat had gone dry and she couldn't manage to utter a sound. This was the moment she'd been waiting for for so long. She and Sebastian were going to be the first people to see the tomb of Telarti.

Hand in hand they stepped forward and peered through the carved doorway. Just beyond the entrance the ground was cracked and uneven and a few large rocks lay at haphazard angles.

'Looks like it isn't the most stable of environments,' Sebastian said, looking at the roof. 'We'll have to tread carefully. One sign of instability and we're out of here.'

Emma nodded but she wasn't really listening. Just a few yards ahead of her, still mainly concealed by the darkness, she could see something on the walls.

Slowly they walked into the entrance of the tomb. Emma gasped as the torches illuminated the walls, showing the detailed paintings and hieroglyphics.

'There are stairs leading down,' Sebastian said, his voice thick with emotion.

Emma knew he had been in Egypt a long time, but she doubted he'd ever laid eyes on anything as beautiful or so well preserved as this tomb, and they'd barely passed the entrance.

Carefully they picked their way down the flight of stairs, stopping every couple of steps to admire the murals.

'Beautiful Companion, Beloved of Mut,' Emma read from one of the walls.

'We're in the right place,' Sebastian said. 'This really is Telarti's tomb.'

'Mistress of Charm, Sweetness and Love,' Emma read a little farther down.

The floor levelled out and Emma glanced behind them. The entrance seemed a long way away and their path was only illuminated by the burning torches. The narrow stairway widened into a chamber with benches along two sides.

Placed on the benches were a variety of bowls and drinking vessels.

'This was where they left the offerings,' Sebastian said, his voice hushed with awe.

Emma walked around the perimeter of the room, staring in disbelief at the vivid colours that covered the walls.

'They're scenes of Telarti travelling through the underworld to meet Osiris,' Emma said as she looked at the pictures she'd seen only in books before now. 'And look at the ceiling—it's beautiful.'

The ceiling was painted a deep, dark blue and was studded with small yellow stars. Emma felt as if her senses were being overwhelmed. She thought she could stay here for ever and be content just looking at the murals.

Sebastian crossed the room and took her hand, a look of awe in his eyes. Silently they moved through the chamber and to the doorway at the end. There was another set of stairs leading downwards, currently completely in darkness.

Emma allowed Sebastian to lead her. With anyone else she might feel a little scared, venturing so deep into the earth with only the flickering torches for illumination, but with Sebastian

by her side Emma felt completely safe. She
knew he wouldn't let any harm come to her.
She felt him squeeze her hand as they began the
second descent and she wondered whether this
would hold the same excitement for her without
Sebastian. She knew the answer immediately.
Although discovering the tomb of Telarti was
exciting in itself, doing it with the man she loved
made it even more special.

They stepped into the burial chamber at the
bottom of the flight of stairs and Emma gasped.
If she'd thought the rest of the tomb was beautiful then this was magnificent. The walls again
were covered in vivid paintings, the pigments
not faded by light and as vibrant as the day they
were painted. As well as the murals the chamber was filled almost from wall to wall with
treasures beyond Emma's wildest imagination.
There were chests of jewellery and piles of or-
nately decorated golden plates and beautiful
stone carvings. Emma didn't know where to
look; every direction was filled with wonders
more impressive than anything she'd ever seen
before.

'I can't…' Sebastian's words trailed off as he
continued his perusal of the room.

Emma knew exactly how he was feeling. All

this history and all these wonders were over-powering.

'In all my time in Egypt I've never seen anything like this,' Sebastian said eventually.

Emma turned to him and looked into his eyes in the flickering torchlight. She knew she had to say something now; she had to make him see he couldn't leave her alone. Everything was better when they did it together, and she had to fight to make him see it.

'Sebastian,' she said, her voice wavering with emotion.

Before she could say any more he moved closer to her and looped an arm around her back. Emma felt him pulling her closer and instinctively held the torch out to one side so she wouldn't get burned. Then her body was pressed up against his and Emma felt the heat radiating from his skin to hers.

Emma opened her mouth to speak again, but Sebastian swooped quickly and captured her lips with his own. She felt all the tension melt from her shoulders as he nipped at her lips and darted his tongue into her mouth.

She nuzzled in closer to him, pressing her body firmly against his, then she let go. She let go of all the thoughts of the future and all the memories of the past couple of weeks. She allowed herself just to live in the moment and savour being here in Telarti's tomb with the man she loved.

After a minute Sebastian pulled away and looked down at her.

'This is incredible,' he said, his voice hoarse.

Emma nodded, not sure whether he was talking about their kiss or the tomb or both.

'Emma, whatever happens in the future, I want you to know these last few weeks have been the best of my life.'

She could see the boyish enthusiasm in his eyes and felt pleased she had helped to put it there.

'I could never have imagined discovering a tomb such as this,' he continued.

Emma felt the smile freeze on her face. Was he just talking about finding the tomb?

'But I would give up discovering a thousand tombs even more magnificent than this for the couple of weeks we spent together.'

Emma felt her heart soar, then immediately plummet back to earth. He was still talking as though some time in the near future they would separate and lead completely independent lives.

'Don't give up on us,' Emma whispered, taking his hand in her own. 'I love you and I know you love me. Don't give up on that.'

Before he could answer her, and before he could see the tears that were building in her eyes, Emma stepped away from him on the pretence of exploring deeper into the burial chamber. Her flickering torch illuminated a pile of scrolls stacked neatly in one corner and Emma crossed the room and eyed them, all the while wondering what was going through Sebastian's mind.

Gently, she ran a finger over the topmost scroll, looking for any sign of fragility in the papyrus, any sign it would disintegrate if she picked it up. It was sturdy beneath her fingers so carefully she picked it up with one hand and started to unroll the stiff papyrus. The markings were hard to see in the torchlight but she peered at them nevertheless, wanting anything to distract her from Sebastian's presence behind her. He hadn't said a word since her entreaty for him not to give up on them, and she wanted to give him time to absorb what she'd said. She wanted to give him a chance to realise the best place for both of them in the future was in each other's arms.

She heard him move a couple of steps and

braced herself for either his arm slipping around her waist or a more formal tap on the shoulder. Seconds passed and neither contact came and Emma realised he'd been moving away from her rather than towards her. She felt the tears well up once again in her eyes and she wondered whether this time she'd lost him for good.

Chapter Thirty-Two

Sebastian took a step towards Emma then thought better of it. He needed to get things clear in his head before he voiced his thoughts. He needed to make a final decision.

He loved her, that much he knew; he loved her more than he'd thought it was possible to love. He wanted her as well. His body thrummed with desire every time she was within touching distance; just thinking about her made him want to lay her down and make love to her until neither of them could think straight.

So he loved her and he desired her, but was that enough? Sebastian shook his head. Surely it didn't matter how much he loved her, he could still end up hurting her. The idea of raising a hand to Emma might seem ludicrous now, but how could he know what the future held?

Images of what could be flickered through

his mind and he saw himself happy with her by his side. He knew if he sent her away he would never be happy again. Every day would be spent pining for her, missing her laugh and her smile, wishing she were back in his arms and knowing he only had himself to blame.

He looked around the tomb and nearly laughed. Four weeks ago discovering a tomb like this would have been his ultimate ambition—now he would give it all up to be able to spend his life with Emma. He'd do anything if it meant spending his life with her by his side.

Seb's eyes rested on an image of the goddess Hathor and silently he beseeched her for guidance. Seb knew the old gods were no longer listening, but he wished the goddess would give him a clue as to what to do. Idly he ran his fingers through a chest of jewellery as he wondered what to do for the best.

'I'll give up this tomb, I'll give up all the treasures and the accolade of discovery, if you just guide me, Hathor,' he whispered.

Gently he felt his shoulders sag at the weight of the decision and as he stared at Emma's back he wondered whether he was about to ruin both their lives for good.

A distant rumble swept all thoughts of the

future from his mind. Instinctively he spun on his heel and peered back the way they'd come. There was nothing there. Just as his heart was beginning to slow another rumble was followed by a crash that shook the ground they stood on.

Emma's eyes met his and the panic he saw in them sliced through his chest. In a couple of quick steps he crossed the room and swept her into his arms. As he pressed her against his body he could feel the pounding of her heart beneath her skin.

'What was that?' Emma asked as another rumble almost drowned her out.

Momentarily Seb didn't know how to answer, then as another rumble shook the tomb he realised what was happening.

'The tunnel's unstable,' he said, remembering the pile of rubble close to the entrance. 'We must have disturbed something coming in.'

Emma's eyes darted to the ceiling of the tomb and Seb saw the panic in them. He too looked up and baulked as he saw the cleft in the rock above their heads. A small shower of stones and dust started to fall and quickly Seb pulled Emma into the doorway of the burial chamber.

'We've got to get out of here,' Seb shouted,

aware that the rumbles were getting closer together.

Emma looked wistfully back into the chamber before reluctantly nodding her head.

'Maybe we should try and take something with us,' she said. 'Save something.'

An image of Emma being crushed underneath a pile of rock made Seb shudder and insistently he pulled her forward.

'No time,' he said. 'We have to get out of here.'

Emma took one last look back over her shoulder then allowed Seb to pull her up the first of the steps. They were just reaching where the ground levelled out at the first set of chambers when an almighty crash reverberated round the enclosed space and the shock almost knocked them off their feet.

Seb felt his blood pulsing through his temples. He had to get Emma out of here and fast. He'd never forgive himself if something happened to her. He just wanted her to be safe in his arms, somewhere nothing could ever hurt her again.

Quickly he led her through the first set of chambers and up the first of the steps that would lead them back into the open air and to safety.

They'd only taken three steps when they were forced to stop. In front of them was a huge pile of rock, almost sealing the tunnel completely. Seb now knew what the loud crash had been: this part of the ceiling of the tunnel had fallen in. Frantically he pulled at the rock, knowing he could never move it all in time to get them out before the entire tunnel came down.

'We can escape up there,' Emma said, pointing to a gap between the pile of rock and the ceiling. It was just about wide enough for one person to squeeze through.

Seb scrambled up the precarious mound of rock and peered through, throwing his torch so it illuminated the other side. Quickly he slid down again and faced Emma.

'It's a sheer drop on the other side. If I get through I'll be able to help you down. Will you be able to scramble up on your own?'

Emma nodded and within a few seconds Seb was back at the top of the pile of rocks, squeezing through the small gap. He felt the sharp edges rip at his clothes and he knew he would have many scrapes and bruises by the end, but it didn't matter. If he managed to get Emma out of here alive he didn't care what injuries he sustained.

Once he was through the gap he braced himself then dropped down, gritting his teeth as he landed on the uneven ground and his feet scrabbled for purchase.

'Come on through,' he shouted.

The wait seemed like an eternity. He could hear Emma on the other side trying to clamber up the pile of rock, but still she did not appear. There was another loud crash and the whole tunnel shook as something collapsed farther down.

'Emma?' he called, frantically hoping she was all right.

No answer.

'Emma,' he called again, panic rising up inside him.

She couldn't be hurt; she couldn't be trapped inside. He needed her with him, by his side, in his arms.

Suddenly her head appeared through the gap and Seb felt his whole body relax a little. He hadn't lost her. She was still alive and in one piece.

'Wriggle through, then I'll catch you,' he instructed.

Emma slowly began to emerge through the

gap until it was just her legs. She looked at him uncertainly.

'How will I get down?' she asked, looking at the drop dubiously.

Seb knew it would be too difficult for her to turn around and lower herself down so he stepped forward and opened his arms.

'Just push yourself forward as hard as you can and I promise I'll catch you.'

He wondered if she would hesitate, if she would trust him or if she would seek another way down.

He saw her eyes fix on his and then she was sailing through the air. Seb opened his arms and braced himself. Emma hit him with quite a force, but he managed to keep his balance, wrapping his arms around her and gently lowering her to the ground.

He knew they had to get out of the tunnel, but he was so happy she hadn't been injured he took a second to brush a kiss against her lips and hold her body tight against his.

Then, before they could be crushed by any more falling rock, he pulled her up the remaining steps and into the sunlight.

They both had to blink over and again when they emerged into the light, and they stood for a minute just looking at the entrance of the tomb. Seb pulled Emma farther back until they were standing just next to the crevice that led them back to the main trail.

As they watched there was another huge rumble and a crash that reverberated round the whole valley. Dust billowed from the entrance to the tomb and for a few seconds they both had to shut their eyes. When Seb opened his he saw the entrance was now completely sealed by another pile of rubble, and he knew if they'd been a minute longer they would have been trapped inside.

He dragged his eyes away from the tomb and looked at Emma. She was pale and dusty, but most importantly she was unhurt. When he had been waiting for her to emerge over the pile of rubble he had thought he might have lost her. The pain he'd felt in his heart had been unbearable. Gently he gathered her in his arms and just pulled her towards him, holding her in an embrace that he never wanted to break.

'I love you,' he whispered into her neck as he held her against himself. 'I love you.'

He felt her relax in his arms and press her face into his shoulder.

'I was so scared I'd lost you,' he said, stroking her hair as he held her. 'I can't live without you.'

Emma stiffened at his words and slowly pulled away so she could look into his eyes.

Seb knew he'd spoken the truth; he couldn't live without her. He couldn't spend every day knowing she was elsewhere, wondering if she was in danger and not being able to protect her. He needed her by his side. He needed her to be his wife.

Emma didn't utter a word, but just looked at him, a wariness in her eyes as if she didn't want to hope too much.

Seb was just about to take her hands in his own when his fingers brushed over a bulge in his pocket. He slipped his hand in and his fingers closed around something cold and it was a few seconds before he realised what it was. In the chamber, just before the first rumble, he'd been running his fingers absent-mindedly through the chest of jewellery. He must have inadvertently slipped a piece of the jewellery into his pocket before they'd fled.

With his eyes locked on hers Seb sank down in front of her and took the ring from his pocket.

'Emma, will you do me the greatest honour of becoming my wife?' he asked.

She was quiet for a second, looking at him warily.

'What kind of wife?' she asked eventually.

Seb grinned. 'A proper wife. A wife who never has to leave her husband's side. A wife who is her husband's partner and whole world.'

He watched as the tears sprang to Emma's eyes and felt a lump start to form in his throat. How could he ever have imagined he'd be able to live his life without her?

'What do you say?' he asked.

'Yes,' Emma replied, leaning down to kiss him on the lips. 'Yes, yes, yes.'

Seb held the ring forward and they both looked at it for the first time.

'Is that…?' Emma's voice trailed off.

'It's a gift from the goddess Hathor,' Seb said, slipping it onto her finger.

Emma studied it carefully and Seb smiled at how perfectly it fitted on her slender finger, as if it had been made just for her. The delicate band held a beautifully cut emerald that glinted in the sunlight.

'We're truly going to be married?' Emma asked.

'Truly.'

'And you won't send me away?'

Seb shook his head. 'I couldn't. My heart wouldn't withstand being apart from you for more than a minute.'

Emma nodded, brushing the tears from her cheeks, and Seb took her hand in his.

'What do we do about the tomb?' she asked.

'I think we've found something much more precious than an old tomb,' Seb said, grinning. 'Why don't we let Telarti keep her secrets for a few years longer?'

He remembered his promise to the goddess. Someone had shown him the way inside the tomb, and, although he knew the ancient gods didn't answer prayers any more, he was going to stick to his end of the bargain nevertheless.

'I love you.'

Seb looked down at the woman who would soon become his wife and he knew his life was complete. He loved her so much.

'Will you promise me something?' he asked, turning serious.

'Anything.'

'If I ever as much as raise my voice to you, you'll leave me.'

Emma looked at him for a long time. She must have realised how much this meant to him, for she nodded solemnly. 'I promise. I know it will never happen, but I promise all the same.'

'I love you more than you could ever know. I love you with all I have,' Seb said, cupping her face in his hands and kissing her leisurely. He had all the time in the world to enjoy lavishing attention on his new wife.

Epilogue

$\mathcal{C}\!\!\sim\!\!\mathcal{O}\!\!\sim\!\!\mathcal{O}\!\!\sim\!\!\mathcal{O}$

Emma wiped her forehead and replaced her wide-brimmed hat. After three years in Egypt she knew she was never going to get rid of the freckles that covered her nose, but she still didn't want the rest of her skin to burn.

She couldn't believe it was three years since she'd first sailed down the Nile, three years since she'd first locked eyes with Sebastian as he dived into the murky waters and surfaced by her felucca. And it was three years since they had discovered the tomb of Telarti.

Emma thought back to their adventure in the desert and smiled. The interceding three years had held their share of adventures, but luckily nothing as perilous as their first foray into the desert together.

It still made her grin when she thought of the nights they'd spent under the stars after discovering the tomb, getting to know each other intimately. At the time she'd never wanted them to end, but Sebastian had been keen to get her back to Cairo and make her his wife. And he'd promised they'd spend many more nights camped out under the stars with just each other for company.

Emma remembered too their arrival back in Cairo. They'd taken the boat from Luxor, and had been joined by Ahmed and Dalila, the Fitzgeralds' maid, before the boat had finally docked in the city centre. Mrs Fitzgerald had been waiting for them at the dock, dragging her hen-pecked husband behind her and looking scandalised and ready for a fight. She hadn't for one minute believed Emma's virtue had been protected and had demanded Sebastian and Emma marry *immediately*.

Sebastian had chortled at that and asked whether she could really deprive the female population of Cairo his charm and attention. Mrs Fitzgerald hadn't even smiled.

The older lady had been mollified slightly when she'd found out Sebastian had already proposed, but she had still whisked Emma away and hadn't let her out of her sight until the wedding day. Thankfully on being separated from his bride-to-be Sebastian had worked like a madman and three days later they had wed. There had of course been the inevitable gossip surrounding the quick marriage, but when they had been comfortably ensconced as husband and wife, that had all died down quickly enough.

They had never revealed the location of Telarti's tomb, instead preferring to keep it a secret between themselves. Sometimes, on long summer evenings, they would talk about going to excavate the tomb again, but Emma knew Sebastian wanted the tomb to remain hidden. He'd made some sort of pact with the goddess down there, and Emma was content to leave it at that.

She straightened up for a few seconds and smiled, looking over to where Sebastian was deep in conversation, pointing out features of the impressive statues that flanked the entrance of the temple.

'But why do they have human heads?' the little voice asked.

'That's just what a sphinx is,' Sebastian replied.

'Could I have the body of a lion?'

Sebastian pretended to consider the question seriously, looking up and down the small form before shaking his head.

'Unfortunately you're not a mythical creature.'

'I'd like some wings, too.'

'Well, that's just being greedy.'

The small boy giggled and Emma watched as Sebastian hoisted his son onto his shoulders and strolled over to where she was crouched.

'Is Daddy distracting you from your excavations, Tom?' Emma asked.

Tom nodded seriously then grabbed a handful of Sebastian's hair.

'Mr Oakfield, you know Tom has a deadline to meet,' Emma said scoldingly. 'He's promised the curate of the museum he'll have a perfect drawing of a sphinx by next week.'

Sebastian pretended to look sheepish and swung his son from his shoulders. He kissed him on the top of the head and told him to go and carry on his drawing.

'What have you found, Mrs Oakfield?' he asked when Tom was contentedly sitting in the shade, drawing the sphinx.

Emma knelt down and started to brush the dust off a broken piece of plaster. She felt Sebastian crouch down beside her. After a few minutes of careful brushing an image started to appear.

'Our old friend Hathor,' Sebastian said with a grin. 'Always watching over us.'

Emma picked up the piece of plaster and studied it. It was beautiful, the colours still so vibrant and the detail meticulous.

'The museum will be pleased,' she said.

'I wonder why they bother commissioning me,' Sebastian said with a grin. 'They could just cut out the middleman and go to the woman with the real talent at finding lost treasures.'

Emma stood, holding her back as she rose.

'Getting old, Mrs Oakfield?' Sebastian asked with a grin, just managing to dodge out of the way of a playful slap in time.

'No, not old,' Emma said cryptically.

She glanced over to where their son was happily entertaining himself amongst the rubble of the temple, making conversation with the stone sphinx.

'I was thinking, with the museum giving us more and more commissions, maybe we should expand the company a little.'

Sebastian pulled a face. 'I don't need anyone but you and Tom,' he said. 'Let the museum wait for their results.'

Emma smiled and pulled Sebastian closer to

her. 'Not even if our new member was another Oakfield?'

Sebastian looked at her for a few seconds before understanding dawned on his face.

'You're not…? We're not…?'

Emma nodded. 'We're bringing another bundle of trouble into the world.'

Sebastian lunged forward and caught her in his arms, picking her up and spinning her round.

'Well, this one can't be as much trouble as that little terror,' Sebastian said, motioning to where Tom was looking up at a half-tumbled-down wall as if considering whether he could climb it.

Emma raised her eyebrows and grinned. 'With a father like you I dread to think what they'll be like.'

Sebastian took her hand and gently brushed a kiss against her lips.

'I do love you, Emma.'

'I love you too.'

'You'll have to stop coming out on the excavations,' Sebastian said, trying to keep a straight face.

'And leave you and Tom to it? I don't think so. Nothing would ever get done.'

Sebastian pulled her towards him and looked

down at her lovingly. As he bent his head to kiss her Emma knew she was one of the lucky ones. She had a wonderful husband and a beautiful little boy, and soon they would have another little Oakfield to complete their family.

* * * * *

MILLS & BOON®
The Italians Collection!

2 BOOKS FREE!

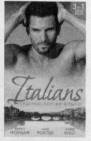

Irresistibly Hot Italians

You'll soon be dreaming of Italy with this scorching six-book collection. Each book is filled with three seductive stories full of sexy Italian men! Plus, if you order the collection today, you'll receive two books free!

This offer is just too good to miss!

Order your complete collection today at
www.millsandboon.co.uk/italians

0815_ST17

MILLS & BOON®

It Started With...Collection!

1 BOOK FREE!

Be seduced with this passionate four-book collection
from top author Miranda Lee. Each book contains
3-in-1 stories brimming with passion and intensely
sexy heroes. Plus, if you order today, you'll get
one book free!

Order yours at
www.millsandboon.co.uk/startedwith

0715_ST15

MILLS & BOON®

The Rising Stars Collection!

1 BOOK
FREE!

This fabulous four-book collection features 3-in-1
stories from some of our talented writers who are the
stars of the future! Feel the temperature rise this
summer with our ultra-sexy and powerful heroes.
Don't miss this great offer—buy the collection
today to get one book free!

**Order yours at
www.millsandboon.co.uk/risingstars**

0715_ST16

MILLS & BOON®

It's Got to be Perfect

* cover in development

When Ellie Rigby throws her three-carat engagement ring into the gutter, she is certain of only one thing. She has yet to know true love!

Fed up with disastrous internet dates and conflicting advice from her friends, Ellie decides to take matters into her own hands. Starting a dating agency, Ellie becomes an expert in love. Well, that is until a match with one of her clients, charming, infuriating Nick, has her questioning everything she's ever thought about love…

**Order yours today at
www.millsandboon.co.uk**

MILLS & BOON®

HISTORICAL

AWAKEN THE ROMANCE OF THE PAST

A sneak peek at next month's titles...

In stores from 4th September 2015:

- **Marriage Made in Shame** – Sophia James
- **Tarnished, Tempted and Tamed** – Mary Brendan
- **Forbidden to the Duke** – Liz Tyner
- **The Rebel Daughter** – Lauri Robinson
- **Her Enemy Highlander** – Nicole Locke
- **The Countess and the Cowboy** – Elizabeth Lane

Available at WHSmith, Tesco, Asda, Eason, Amazon and Apple

Just can't wait?
Buy our books online a month before they hit the shops!
visit www.millsandboon.co.uk

These books are also available in eBook format!

0815/04